AMERICAN ENGLISH CONVERSATION IN SIX WEEKS

by Tina Lin
   Mark A. Pengra

LEARNING PUBLISHING CO., LTD.

編者的話

您是否也有同樣的經驗——

好不容易裝上小耳朵（ *Satellite Disk* ），打開電視，想要接收最新資訊，欣賞高水準的節目，但是，嘰哩呱啦一連串的美語，令您望之乏味呢？興沖沖地出國旅遊，想要博覽山水，增廣見聞，但是，語言溝通困難，使您寸步難行，敗興而歸呢？

美語，在今天不僅是世界共通的語言，也漸漸成為我們生活語言的一部分。本公司針對此時代的需要，特邀中外編輯，將美語的會話精華編成「**六週美語會話**」（ *American English Conversation in Six Weeks* ）一書，教您如何簡化美語的學習過程，在最短的時間內，達到最高的效果。使您在六週之內，輕輕鬆鬆地說一口流利的美語。

本書經過精心設計，每一部分都能切中您的語言需要，其內容主要有三大特色：

一、有計劃有系統的編排

由淺入深、循序漸進地分成三十六個單元，一天學一個單元，六天為一階段。從最基本的會話到完全靈活運用，您只須花六週的時間，就可以開口和老外打成一片。

< 🎤 六週美語會話 >

二、生動活潑的對話內容

在" **BASIC DIALOGUES** "中,有該單元最常用的基礎用法。在" **APPLIED CONVERSATION** "中,作實際模擬的應用對話。使您在富有臨場感的會話中,自然而然地脫口說美語。

三、詳盡的注釋和解說

在" **HINT BANK** "中,將較深的字彙——註解加上標音,將較難的詞句,作淺顯易懂的說明,加強您對美語用字遣詞的印象。

這是個知識爆炸的時代,您需要有輕、薄、短小,隨時可以消化,隨時可以吸收的好書。「六週美語會話」即根據您的需要編寫而成。本書從編寫、撰稿到校對,均力求完善,但恐仍有疏漏之處,敬祈各界先進不吝指正。

Editorial Staff

● 企劃・編著／林　婷
● 英文撰稿

　Mark A. Pengra・Bruce S. Stewart

　Edward C. Yulo・John C. Didier
● 校訂

　劉　毅・葉淑霞・武藍蕙・王怡華・王慶銘

　曾蕙藺・陳怡平・林順隆・陳威如・陳斯如
● 校閱

　Mark A. Pengra・Lois M. Findler

　John H. Voelker・Keith Gaunt
● 封面設計／謝淑敏
● 版面設計／謝淑敏・張鳳儀
● 版面構成／

　黃春蓮・蘇翠鳳・許仲綺・林麗鳳
● 打字

　黃淑貞・倪秀梅・蘇淑玲・吳秋香

　洪桂美・徐湘君
● 校對

　黃惠美・林韶慧・陳瑠琍・陳玉美

　邱蔚樊・卓永堅・劉宛淯・朱輝錦

AMERICAN ENGLISH
CONVERSATION IN SIX WEEKS
CONTENTS

第 1 週  日常基礎會話

第2週 基本用法表達

第3週 應答重點的強調

第4週　談話內容的敍述

第6週　與熟識的英美朋友聊天

學習出版公司　港澳地區版權顧問

RM ENTERPRISES

P.O. Box 99053 Tsim Sha Tsui Post Office, Hong Kong

翻印必究

日常基礎會話

1st Week Basic Expressions In Everyday Conversation

First Week, First Day

Greetings on Meeting and Parting

第一週‧第一天　碰面與道別的問候語

BASIC DIALOGUES

1. A : *Good morning*, Mr. Smith. 早安，史密斯先生。

   B : Good morning, Mr. Lee. 早安，李先生。

2. A : Good afternoon, Mr. Baker. 午安，貝克爾先生。

   B : Good afternoon, Mary. 午安，瑪麗。

3. A : Good evening, John. 晚安，約翰。

   B : Good evening, David. 晚安，大衞。

4. A : Hello, Bill. 嗨，比爾。

   B : Hello, Mei-mei. 嗨，美美。

5. A : How are you, Mr. Wang ? 王先生，你好嗎？

   B : *Quite well*, Mr. Brown. And you ?

   　　很好，布朗先生，你呢？

   A : Just fine, thank you. 很好，謝謝。

6. A： *It's so nice to see you again*, Henry. 亨利，很高興再次見到你。

 B： It's been a long time, hasn't it? 好久（不見）了，不是嗎？

 A： I should say so. Have you been well? 說的是，你一向都好嗎？

 B： Yes, quite well, thank you. 是的，很好，謝謝你。

7. A： Goodbye, Mr. Jones.

 瓊斯先生，再見。

 B： Goodbye, Mr. Yeh.

 葉先生，再見。

8. A： *Good night*, Jim. 吉姆，晚安。

 B： Good night, Lily. 晚安，莉莉。

9. A： *So long*, Tina. 再見，婷娜。

 B： So long, Fred. See you in the morning.

 再見，弗雷德。（明天）早上見。

10. A： *I must be going* now. 現在我得走了。

 B： Really? Can't you stay a bit longer?

 眞的？不能再多呆一會兒嗎？

 A： No, I really must go. 不，我眞的得走了。

11. A： I hope I'll be able to see you again soon. 希望能很快再見到你。

 B： I certainly hope so, too. 當然我也是這麼希望。

HINT BANK————————————

 ＊" Good evening." 這句寒喧語，適用於傍晚或晚上的打招呼。"Good night."
 則是在夜晚道別時用，所以，有「再見」的意思。

 ＊" Quite well." 是" I'm quite well." 的省略用法，是較輕鬆隨便的講法。

 ＊" It's so nice to see you." 「很高興再次見到你。」" It's been" 是" It has
 been" 的省略。" I should say so." 是表示同意的講法。

 ＊" So long." 是" Goodbye." 的通俗用語。" in the morning" 是指明天早上。

◀ APPLIED CONVERSATION ▶ 在街上遇見朋友

Meeting a Friend on the Street

中國人：Good morning, Mr. Brown.
　　　　早安，布朗先生。

外國人：Oh, good morning, Mr. Lee.
　　　　喔，早安，李先生。

中國人：*How have you been*？近來好嗎？

外國人：Fine, thank you. And how is your wife？很好，謝謝。你太太好嗎？

中國人：She *came down with the flu*, but she's much better now, thank you. 她感冒了，不過她現在好多了，謝謝你。

外國人：Well, I'm glad to hear that. 嗯，我很高興聽你那麼說。

中國人：And *how is everyone at your house*？你的家人都好嗎？

外國人：Quite well, thank you. I'm meeting my wife and daughter for lunch at 12 o'clock. Would you *care to* join us？
　　　　很好，謝謝你。我十二點要跟我的太太和女兒會面吃午飯。要不要一道去？

中國人：*I'd love to*, but I'm afraid I can't. I already have a luncheon engagement.
　　　　我很樂意，不過恐怕不能，我午餐已經有約了。

HINT BANK ──────────────

· *come down with* 患（病）；得　　luncheon〔ˈlʌntʃən〕*n.*（特指正式的）午餐

* "I am glad to hear that." 是用在聽到好消息時，所做的回答。

* "Would you～?" 是表示禮貌委婉的詢問。"care" 和 "like" 的意思類似，有「想要」的意思。

外國人：Well, then, perhaps we can get together another time.

嗯，那麼，也許我們可以再找個時間聚一聚。

中國人：I hope so, too. 我也希望如此。

外國人：*I wonder if* you and Mrs. Lee will be free next Friday evening？

不知道你和你（李）太太下週五晚上是否有空？

中國人：Friday？ That's the 15th, isn't it？ Yes, we are free that evening.

星期五？那就是15日，不是嗎？是的，那天晚上我們有空。

外國人：Well, we're having a few friends in for dinner, and we'd like you and your wife to join us.

嗯，我們有幾個朋友來家裏吃晚餐，我們希望你和你太太能一道來。

中國人：That's very kind of you, Mr. Brown. We would enjoy that very much. But I should *check with* my wife first. I'll call you tomorrow.

布朗先生，你真好。我們很樂於到貴府吃飯。不過，我要先問我太太一聲，明天我會打電話給您。

外國人：*Sure thing*. I think I'd better be *running along*. My wife is waiting for me. Which way are you going？

當然。我不得不走了。我太太在等我。你走哪條路？

HINT BANK──────────────

- *check with* 確定；問問看　　*sure thing* 〔美口〕的確；必然；當然
- *run along* 〔俗〕走開；離開（＝ *go away*；*be off*）

* "We're having a few in for dinner." 這是表示「招待幾位朋友到家裏吃飯。」用進行式是指未來即將發生的事。用 "in" 是指「到家裏」。
* "would like ～ to …" 是表示「希望～做…」的句型。

中國人：I'm taking the bus. And you?

　　　　我要搭巴士，你呢？

外國人：I have only *a short distance* to go, so I think I'll walk.

　　　　我要去的地方只有很短的距離，所以我想我會用走的。

中國人：I'm glad I *ran into* you today. 很高興今天遇見你。

外國人：*I'm looking forward to* hearing from you tomorrow.

　　　　希望明天得到你的消息。

中國人：I'll be sure to call, Mr. Brown.

　　　　我一定會打電話的，布朗先生。

外國人：Goodbye, Mr. Lee. 李先生，再見。

中國人：Goodbye. *Remember me to* Mrs. Brown.

　　　　再見。請代我向布朗太太問候。

外國人：I certainly will. 我一定會的。

HINT BANK

- *run into* 偶遇；碰見　　*hear from* 得到～的消息

* " I'm looking forward to～. " 用在表示「快樂的期待或等待」。 " to " 之後接動名詞。

* " Remember me to～. " 這是請別人「代我向～問候」。

Grammar and Usage

1. 用現在進行式表示預定的未來

進行式（be 動詞＋現在分詞），本來是表示動作正在進行。但是在會話中，常以現在進行式來表示預定的未來。例如：

- *I'm going to meet* them for lunch at 12 o'clock.
  （我將在十二點和他們會面吃午餐。）
- *We're going to have* a few friends in for dinner.
  （我們將有幾個朋友來家裏吃晚餐。）

在會話中，通常直接用現在進行式來表示，如下：

- *I'm meeting* them for lunch at 12 o'clock.
- *We're having* a few friends in for dinner.

如果是在文章中，只有表示「往來、出發、到達」的動詞，才可以用現在進行式來代替未來式，如：" come "，" leave "，" start "，" arrive "等動詞。

2. 會話的開場白

我們中國人在路上遇見朋友，常會喜歡問對方：「你要去哪裏？」但是，這對外國人來說，就是不太禮貌的對話方式。問對方："Where are you going？"已經涉及到對方的隱私權，最好不要隨便亂問。

最普遍的會話開場白是，問有關對方的健康情形，如：

- *How are you*？（你好嗎？）
- *How have you been*？（你近況如何？）

其他，有關氣候的話題，也可以用來當作
會話的開場白。

First Week, Second Day

Introducing and Being Introduced

第一週，第二天　介紹與被介紹

BASIC DIALOGUES

1. A : Mr. Brown, *this is* Mr. Wang. 布朗先生，這位是王先生。

B : How do you do, Mr. Brown? 你好嗎，布朗先生？

C : *It's a pleasure to meet you*, Mr. Wang.
很榮幸認識你，王先生。

2. A : Mr. Smith, I'd like you to meet Miss Lily Wu.
史密斯先生，我跟你介紹吳莉莉小姐。

B : It's so nice to meet you, Miss Wu.
很高興認識你，吳小姐。

C : I'm very happy to meet you, Mr. Smith.
很高興認識你，史密斯先生。

3. A : Margaret, this is Fred Carter. 瑪格麗特，這位是弗雷德·卡特。

B : I'm glad to meet you, Fred. 很高興認識你，弗雷德。

C : *Pleased to meet you*, Margaret. I've heard so much
about you. 很榮幸認識你，瑪格麗特。久仰大名。

4. A : *May I introduce myself*? I'm Robert Jones.

　　　請容我介紹自己。我是羅伯特‧瓊斯。

　　B : Mr. Jones? It's a pleasure. I'm David Chang.

　　　瓊斯先生嗎?幸會，我是張大衞。

　　A : I'm very glad to know you, Mr.Chang.

　　　很高興認識你，張先生。

5. A : Have you met Dr. Moore, George ?

　　　喬治，你見過莫爾博士嗎?

　　B : No, *I don't believe I've had the pleasure.*

　　　沒有，我不以爲自己有這個榮幸。

　　A : Dr. Moore, this is my cousin, George Carter.

　　　莫爾博士，這是我表弟，喬治‧卡特。

　　C : *My pleasure*, Mr. Carter. 幸會，卡特先生。

　　B : It's an honor to know you, Dr. Moore.

　　　認識你是一種榮幸，莫爾博士。

HINT BANK————————————————

* 使用在介紹上的固定用語是 " This is ~ ." (這位是…。)初見面時，最常用的寒喧語是 " How do you do." 另外，也可以用 "It's a pleasure to meet you."

* 爲別人介紹某人時，用 " I'd like you to meet ~ ." 的句型。

* " It's so nice to meet you." (很高興認識你。)和 " I'm very happy to meet you." 的意思相同。

* " Have you met ~ ? " 不只問「是否見過…?」，也是指「是否被人介紹過…?」

* " My pleasure." 是指 " It's my pleasure to meet you."

⫸ APPLIED CONVERSATION ⫷ 宴會上的介紹
Introductions at a Party

中國人1：I'm so glad you were able to come, George. I believe you know most of the people here.
喬治，很高興你能來。我想這裏的人你大部分都認識。

喬 治：Yes, I think I do. Oh, there's Harry Foster. *Let me go over and see him.*
是的，我想是的。喔，亨利‧佛斯特在那裏。我過去見見他。

中國人1：Yes, do that, George, but why don't you *get yourself a drink first*?
是的，喬治，過去見見他，不過何不先喝一杯？

喬 治：Hello, Harry. *Long time no see.*
嗨，亨利，好久不見。

亨 利：Why, hello, George. It's good to see you. Have you met Mr. Lin？嗳呀！嗨，喬治，幸會。你見過林先生嗎？

喬 治：No, I don't believe I have. 沒有，我想我沒見過。

HINT BANK————————

· why〔hwaɪ〕*int*.（意外的發現、承認等的驚訝聲）嗳呀！哦！真的！

* "Why don't you ~？"（你何不~？）是用來「鼓勵、勸誘對方」的用語。

* 英語中有一些講法受到中文的影響，像" Long time no see."（好久不見。）這句話已經是美國人很口語化的打招呼用語。

亨　利 ： Mr. Lin, I'd like to introduce George Miller. Mr.
Miller is a business associate of our host.
林先生，我跟你介紹喬治‧米勒先生。米勒先生是我們主
人生意上的夥伴。

中國人2 ： I'm very happy to meet you, Mr. Miller.
很高興認識你，米勒先生。

喬　治 ： *The pleasure is mine*, Mr. Lin. 這是我的榮幸，林先生。

亨　利 ： Mr. Lin is on the engineering staff of the Taiwanese
Computer Company.
林先生在台灣電腦公司的工程部做事。

喬　治 ： Is that right? 是這樣嗎？

中國人2 ： Mr. Miller, *may I present to you* the chief of our
engineering department? Mr. Miller, this is Mr. Chou.
米勒先生，我向你介紹敝公司工程部的主管好嗎？米勒先
生，這位是周先生。

中國人3 ： I'm happy to have the chance to meet you, Mr. Miller.
米勒先生，很高興有這個機會認識你。

喬　治 ： May I *compliment* you *on* your fine office computers?
You know, we've purchased quite a number of them
for export to the United States.
請容我誇讚貴公司出產的品質精良電腦。你知道，我們已
經購買了很多貴公司的電腦，外銷到美國。

HINT BANK ─────────────────

· associate〔ə'soʃɪ,et〕*n.* 夥伴；同事　　staff〔stæf,stɑf〕*n.* 職員的總稱
· *compliment sb. on sth.* 讚美某人某事　　*quite a number of* 相當多
* "May I present to you" 中的 " present " 有 " introduce " 的意思。

中國人3：Why, thank you very much. 噯呀，非常謝謝你。

中國人2：Oh, Mr. Foster, ***will you excuse me a moment***？ I'd like to speak to Mr. Johnson. He's over there.

　　　　喔，佛斯特先生，我失陪一會兒。我想和詹森先生說話，他在那裏。

亨　利：Why, certainly. 唔，當然。

中國人2：I'll be right back. 我馬上回來。

中國人3：***By the way***, Mr. Miller, would you like to meet Mr. Liu of our Ministry of Trade and Industry？

　　　　順便一提，米勒先生，你想不想見本公司商務暨產業部的劉先生？

喬　治：Yes, indeed. And I'm sure Mr. Foster would like to meet him, too. 是的，的確，我相信佛斯特先生也想見見他。

中國人3：Excuse me, Mr. Liu, ***I'd like you to meet*** two of our American business friends. This is Mr. Miller, and this is Mr. Foster.

　　　　對不起，劉先生，我希望你見見這兩位跟我們有生意往來的美國朋友。這位是米勒先生，這位是佛斯特先生。

喬　治：***I'm honored***, Mr. Liu. 這是我的榮幸，劉先生。

HINT BANK————————————————

* 表示「暫時離席或離開」時，用" Will you excuse me a moment？"其中" a moment"是指「短暫的時間」。

* 表示「我馬上回來。」在會話中常使用" I'll be right back."和" I'll come right back."

* " by the way"是用來「改變話題」的用語。

* " I'm honored."（我很榮幸。）是較正式的表達方式。

亨　利 ： I believe we met at Mr. Barnett's cocktail party about
　　　　two weeks ago.

　　　　我想，大約兩個禮拜以前，我們在巴尼特先生雞尾酒會上
　　　　見過面。

中國人4： Why, of course. Mr. Foster. How are you? It's nice
　　　　to see you again.

　　　　啊，是啊。佛斯特先生，你好嗎？眞高興再度見到你。

亨　利 ： The pleasure is mine, Mr. Liu.
　　　　這是我的榮幸，劉先生。

HINT BANK ───────────

- *cocktail party*　雞尾酒會（通常地下午四至六點左右舉行的社交聚會，飲食雞
尾酒與各種點心類）

* "I believe ～."並沒有很強烈「相信」的意思，而是表示和"think"意思一
樣的語氣，在會話中常使用這句型。

◢ First Week, Third Day ◣

How to Thank Someone

第一週，第三天　如何致謝

▶ BASIC DIALOGUES ◀

1. A : Thank you. 謝謝你 。

B : *You're welcome*. 不客氣 。

2. A : Thank you very much. 非常謝謝你 。

B : *Not at all*. 那裏！那裏！

3. A : Thanks a lot. 多謝 。

B : Don't mention it. 不要客氣 。

4. A : Thanks. 謝謝 。

B : That's okay. 不客氣 。

5. A : Thank you for your help. 謝謝你的幫忙 。

B : It's a pleasure, sir. 這是我的榮幸 ，先生 。

6. A : I'm deeply indebted to you. 我深深感激你 。

B : Please think nothing of it. 不客氣 。

7. **A :** *I am very grateful to you* for your kindness.
對你的親切，我非常感激。

B : It was nothing at all. 不客氣。

8. **A :** Mr. Lee asked me to convey his thanks to you.
李先生要我轉達他對你的謝意。

B : That was very thoughtful of him. Please give him my best regards. 他眞是體貼。請代我向他問候。

9. **A :** Please accept this as a token of our appreciation and thanks. 請接受這個，作爲我們感激和謝意的表徵。

B : That's very kind of you, sir. 非常感激你，先生。

10. **A :** I'm most grateful for your help, Mr. Smith.
史密斯先生，對你的幫助，我不勝感激。

B : I'm glad I could be of assistance. 我很高興能幫得上忙。

11. **A :** I appreciate everything you've done for us.
我很感激你爲我們所做用一切。

B : You're quite welcome. It was a pleasure.
哪兒的話，這是一種榮幸。

HINT BANK─────────────

• indebted〔ɪnˈdɛtɪd〕*adj.* 有恩的；受恩的　　convey〔kənˈve〕*v.* 傳達；表達
• thoughtful〔ˈθɔtfəl〕*adj.* 體貼的；（爲他人）設想周到的
• token〔ˈtokən〕*n.* 表徵；標記（= *mark* ; *sign* ）

＊表示「不客氣」的用法中，" You're welcome." 是美式講法，" Not at all."
和 " Don't mention it." 是英式講法。

＊ " I could be of assistance." 是表示「我能有所幫助」的意思，可以用 " be of help" 來替換 " be of assistance "。

◄APPLIED CONVERSATION► 被邀請吃晚餐
Being Invited to Supper

中 國 人：Good evening, Mrs. Johnson.
　　　　Thanks a lot for inviting me.
　　　　詹森太太，晚安。非常謝謝你
　　　　邀請我。

詹森太太：Not at all, Mei-mei. It's a
　　　　pleasure to have you with us.
　　　　不客氣，美美。真高興有你和
　　　　我們在一起。

華 爾 特：Hi, Mei-mei. Glad you could come.
　　　　嗨，美美，很高興你能來。

中 國 人：Hi, Walter. Thanks for inviting me.
　　　　嗨，華爾特，謝謝你邀請我。

詹森太太：Come in and take off your things. Carol and Helen
　　　　are in the other room.
　　　　請進，並請脫去你的外套。卡洛和海倫在另一個房間。

華 爾 特：Here, let me take your coat. 來，我幫你拿外套。

中 國 人：Thanks. 謝謝。

HINT BANK───────────────

- *take off* 脫去（帽子、衣服、鞋等，相反詞是 put on ）
- coat〔kot〕*n.* 上衣；外套；短大衣（通常指和褲、裙相對的上衣）

＊在被別人邀請時，常用的一句感謝話是 " Thanks a lot for inviting me."
＊打招呼時，用 " Hi " 比用 " Hello " 更輕鬆且不拘泥。
＊ " take off your things " 的 " things " 是指「穿在身上的衣服」。

卡　　洛：Hello, Mei-mei. *Where've you been*? We were expecting you earlier.

　　　　　嗨，美美，你到哪裏去了？我們期待你早點來。

中國人：Hello, Carol. Oh, hello, Helen. *I was delayed by traffic*. Sorry I'm late.

　　　　　嗨，卡洛。喔，嗨，海倫。交通阻塞使我延誤了，抱歉我遲到了。

海　　倫：Say, Mei-mei, thanks a lot for dinner the other day. I had a wonderful time.

　　　　　嘿，美美，非常謝謝幾天前的晚餐，我過得非常愉快。

中國人：Not at all. I had a good time, too.

　　　　　那裏！那裏！我也很愉快。

華 爾 特：All right, everyone. Please go into the dining room. Mother says supper is ready.

　　　　　好的，各位，請到餐廳。媽媽說晚飯準備好了。

海　　倫：Great! *I'm starving*. 好極了！我餓死了。

卡　　洛：So am I. 我也是。

詹森太太：Come in, everybody, and take your seats. Walter, *who sits where*? 進來，各位，請坐。華爾特，座位怎麼安排？

HINT BANK

- say〔se〕*n.*〔美口〕喂；嘿；我說…（＝ *I say*〔英口〕）
- *dining room* 飯廳；餐廳
- supper〔ˈsʌpɚ〕*n.* 晚餐；晚飯（尤指比 *dinner* 簡單的餐點）

＊年輕人在高興地表示「好極了！」常用 "Great!"，反而不喜歡用 "Wonderful!"。

＊詢問全部人員的座位順序時，用 "Who sits where？"（座位如何安排？）

華 爾 特：Helen, you sit next to Mei-mei, and Carol, you sit next to me.

海倫，你坐在美美旁邊。卡洛，你坐在我旁邊。

海　　倫：My！ The food certainly looks good. Walter has been telling us *what a good cook you are*, Mrs. Johnson.

哇！菜看起來眞棒。詹森太太，華爾特已經告訴我們，你做的菜有多高明。

詹森太太：Why, thank you, Helen. I hope you like it.

哦！謝謝你，海倫，希望你會喜歡。

卡　　洛：Mei-mei, will you pass me the salt？

美美，請把鹽遞過來好嗎？

中 國 人：Sure, Carol. 當然，卡洛。

卡　　洛：Thanks. 謝謝。

詹森太太：Would you all like coffee or tea？

各位是喜歡咖啡，還是喜歡茶？

中 國 人：Coffee, please. 請來咖啡。

詹森太太：*How about you*, Helen？ 海倫，你呢？

海　　倫：Tea for me, if it isn't too much trouble.

我要茶，如果不會很費事的話。

HINT BANK────────────────

* "My！"是女性表示驚訝的感歎詞，表「哎呀；哎喲；乖乖；天呀」和"My goodness！", "My eye！", "Oh, my！"的意思相同。

* 在端菜或送禮物給別人時，常用的一句話是"I hope you like it."

* 在西洋的禮儀中，通常不伸手拿在別人面前的東西，而是請別人幫忙遞過來，所以，常用"Will you pass me～？"句型。

詹森太太：Not at all. Carol？哪兒的話。卡洛呢？

卡　　洛：I'll have tea too, thank you. 我也要喝茶，謝謝你。

詹森太太：You'll have coffee, won't you, Walter？
　　　　　華爾特，你要喝咖啡，不是嗎？

華　爾　特：Yes, Mother. Thanks. 是的，媽咪，謝謝。

First Week, Fourth Day

How to Express Excuses and Regrets

第一週，第四天　如何道歉和表示惋惜

BASIC DIALOGUES

1. A : Excuse me. 對不起（請原諒）。
   B : That's all right. 沒關係。

2. A : I'm sorry. 抱歉。
   B : Never mind. 不要緊。

3. A : *I beg your pardon*. 請原諒（對不起）。
   B : That's OK. 沒關係。

4. A : I'm so sorry. 非常抱歉。
   B : It doesn't matter. 不要緊。

5. A : Forgive me. 請原諒。
   B : Sure. Forget it. 當然，算了。

6. A : I do hope you'll forgive me. 我真的很希望你會原諒我。
   B : Don't worry about it. 別擔心。

7. A : I was so careless. I'm so sorry. 我太不小心了，眞是抱歉。

　　B : That's all right. *It couldn't be helped*.
　　　　　沒關係，那是無法避免的事情。

8. A : It was rude of me（to do that）. 我（這樣做）眞是失敬。

　　B : It's all right. 沒關係。

9. A : I want to tell you how sorry I am.
　　　　　我想告訴你我有多麼抱歉。

　　B : I understand. Please forget about it. 我了解，不要緊的。

10. A : Can you ever forgive me? 你究竟會不會原諒我？

　　B : Of course. Please don't think anymore about it.
　　　　　當然，請別掛意。

11. A : I'm sorry. I didn't mean to interfere.
　　　　　抱歉，我無意干擾。

　　B : That's all right. 沒關係。

12. A : I'm sorry. I'm afraid *I was mistaken*.
　　　　　抱歉，恐怕我弄錯了。

　　B : Don't worry about it. Anyone can make mistakes.
　　　　　別擔心，任何人都會犯錯。

HINT BANK ───────────────

• careless〔'kɛrlɪs〕*adj.* 不小心的　　interfere〔͵ɪntə'fɪr〕*v.* 妨礙；干擾

＊ "Never mind." 是表示「沒關係；不要緊；不要介意」，更正式的講法是
　 "Don't mention it."

＊ 對於無心所犯的小過錯、失禮等表示歉意時，用 "I beg your pardon." 語尾音
　 調要往下降。

＊ "I was mistaken." 雖然句型上是被動，但是意思卻是表示主動的「我錯了。」

◀ APPLIED CONVERSATION ▶ 朋友住院

A Friend in the Hospital

中國人：Hi, Frank. *How's everything*?
嗨，法蘭克，近來如何？

外國人：Not so good, Allen. Martha's
in the hospital.
不怎麼好，艾倫。瑪莎住院了。

中國人：No! Really? I'm so sorry to
hear that. What happened?
哦不，眞的嗎？聽到這個消息，
眞是遺憾。發生了什麼事？

外國人：She was walking home from the bus stop when a motorcycle hit her.
她從公車站走路回家的時候，有輛摩托車撞到她了。

中國人：*That's terrible*. I hope she wasn't badly hurt.
眞糟糕，希望她沒有傷得很重。

外國人：Both legs were broken. 兩條腿都斷了。

中國人：Gosh, *that's a shame*. You must be busy now.
唉，太可憐啦！你現在一定很忙。

HINT BANK

- gosh〔gɑʃ〕*int*.（表驚愕）唉；哎呀（是 God 的婉轉語，= *by gosh*）

* "That's terrible." 有「眞倒楣，眞糟糕」的意思，和 "That's too bad." 的
意思相同。

* "That's a shame." 的意思有(1)多麼可恨的事！太狠心啦！(2)太可憐啦！太可惜啦！

外國人：Yes. Every evening I'm at the hospital. Martha was *feeling pretty blue* for a while, but she's better now.

　　　　是的，我每天晚上都在醫院。有一陣子瑪莎覺得相當沮喪，不過她現在好多了。

中國人：I'm glad to hear that. Was the driver of the motorcycle injured?

　　　　聽到這樣我很高興。騎摩托車的人有沒有受傷？

外國人：No. He got off without a scratch. To make matters worse, he hasn't even said he's sorry.

　　　　沒有，他下了車，連擦傷也沒有。更糟的是，他甚至連抱歉都沒說。

中國人：I would think it would be pretty hard to forgive someone who acts like that.

　　　　我想要原諒做出這種事來的人，是相當困難的。

外國人：It's hard for me. I don't know why these fool kids buy such big motorcycles — they are dangerous for everyone, including themselves.

　　　　對我來說很難。我不知道爲什麼這些傻孩子買這麼大的摩托車——這種大摩托車對每個人來說，包括他們自己在內，都很危險。

中國人：Have you seen him since the accident?

　　　　從這次意外事故以後，你看過他嗎？

HINT BANK——————————————

• blue〔blu〕*adj.* 憂鬱的；沮喪的　　　scratch〔skrætʃ〕*n.* 擦傷；刮傷

＊ " to make matters worse " 表示「更糟的是」，和 "（and）what is worse" 的意思相同。

外國人：No. His father came to my office and apologized for the boy, but I don't know how the boy feels about it. 沒有，他父親到我的辦公室，爲這個男孩道歉，不過我不知道這個男孩對這個意外的感覺如何。

中國人：How long will Martha be in the hospital？ 瑪莎要住院多久？

外國人：The doctors say at least a month. 醫生們說至少要一個月。

中國人：I'm sorry *I didn't contact you*, Frank. Maybe I could have helped. 法蘭克，抱歉，我沒跟你連絡，也許我幫得上忙。

外國人：That's OK. I know you've been busy. Why don't you *drop by and pay Martha a visit*？ She would appreciate it. 沒關係，我知道你一向很忙。何不順路去看看瑪莎，她會很感激的。

中國人：I will. I'll see if I can make it this evening. Where is she？ 我會的，我看看今天晚上是否能去，她在哪裏？

外國人：Mercy Hospital. Room 218. 慈恩醫院，二一八號病房。

中國人：Thanks, Frank. Goodbye. 謝謝，法蘭克。再見。

外國人：So long, Allen. 再見，艾倫。

HINT BANK————————————

- contact〔kən'tækt〕*v.*〔俗〕與人聯繫；與人接觸
- *drop by* 順便拜訪　　*pay sb. a visit* 拜訪某人
- *So long*〔口〕再見；再會（＝ *good-bye*）

Grammar and Usage

1. *I'm sorry* 的各種用法

表示「對不起」的 " I'm sorry " 可以單獨使用，也可以接子句。如：

· I'm sorry I kept you waiting.（對不起，讓你久等了。）

· I'm sorry that my pronunciation is very bad.
（對不起，我的發音很差。）

· I'm sorry to be late.（對不起，我遲到了。）

" sorry " 除了表示「對不起」的後悔、抱歉的心情之外，也有「惋惜、遺憾」的意思。如：

· I'm sorry to hear about your failure.
（聽到你失敗了，我覺得很難過。）

· I'm sorry to hear that.（我很遺憾聽到這事。）

2. 注意音調

所謂音調（ *intonation* ），就是指聲音的抑揚頓挫。在英文中有音調改變，意思就不一樣的句子。" *I beg your pardon.* " 就是最具代表性的句子。

" *I beg your pardon* ↘ . " 在語尾音調下降，是表示「非常抱歉」的意思，和 " I'm sorry. " 的意思相同。

" *I beg your pardon* ↗ ? " 在語尾音調上升，是表示「請再講一遍」的意思。

◢ First Week Fifth Day ◣

When You Have Not Understood Clearly

第一週，第五天 當你不太明白時

◤ BASIC DIALOGUES ◥

1. **A** : Have you ever been to Frisco? 你去過舊金山嗎？

   B : *I beg your pardon*? 對不起，請再說一次。

   A : Have you ever visited San Francisco? 你去過舊金山嗎？

   B : No, I haven't. 不，我沒有去過。

2. **A** : I'm sorry, I couldn't quite *catch what you were saying*.
      對不起，我不大聽得懂你在說什麼。

   B : Did I speak too rapidly? 我是不是說話太快了。

3. **A** : Could you repeat that, please? 請你再說一遍好嗎？

   B : Yes, certainly. 好的，當然可以。

4. **A** : Will you say that once again? 麻煩你再說一遍好嗎？

   B : Surely. 當然。

5. **A** : What did you say? 你說什麼？

   B : Let me repeat it. 我再重覆一次。

6. A： I'm sorry, I didn't understand you. 抱歉，我不懂你的意思。

　　B： All right, I'll repeat it. 好的，我再重覆一次。

7. A： *Did you get what I said*? 你聽懂我說的嗎？

　　B： No. I'm afraid I didn't. Will you please say it again?
　　　　不，恐怕沒聽懂。請再說一次好嗎？

8. A： *Would you please* speak more slowly? 請你說慢一點好嗎？

　　B： Of course. I'm sorry if I spoke too fast.
　　　　好的，抱歉，我說得太快了。

9. A： I'm afraid you're speaking too rapidly for me to catch
　　　　what you're saying. 恐怕你說得太快了，我聽不懂你在說什麼。

　　B： Oh, I'm sorry. I'll try to speak a little more slowly.
　　　　喔，對不起。我會再說慢一點。

　　A： And could you speak a little louder, please?
　　　　而且，能請你說大聲一點嗎？

　　B： Sure. 當然。

10. A： I'm afraid I don't understand English too well. Could
　　　　you please use simpler words?
　　　　很遺憾我不大懂英文，可否請你用簡單一點的字？

　　B： OK. I'll try to speak *as clearly and simply as possible*.
　　　　好的，我會設法儘可能說得既清楚又簡單。

HINT BANK ─────────────────

- Frisco 〔ˊfrɪsko〕*n.* 〔美俚〕舊金山（ = *San Fransisco*）
- catch 〔kætʃ〕*v.* 聽取；了解

* 問別人「有沒有到過～？」的句型是 "Have you ever been to～?"
* "I beg your pardon?" 表示「對不起，請再說一遍」的意思，用在沒聽懂對方
　的話時。說時把語尾音調上揚。

⟨ APPLIED CONVERSATION ⟩ 請對方再説一遍

Asking One to Repeat

外國人：Good evening. You're Mr. Lee,
aren't you?

晚安，你是李先生，不是嗎？

中國人：Yes, and I believe you're Mr.
Smith.

是的，我想你是史密斯先生。

外國人：That's right. I think *I had the pleasure of meeting you* about a year ago at Mr. John Baker's home.

對，我想，大約一年前在約翰・貝克爾先生家裏，我就有
這個榮幸跟你見過面了。

中國人：Excuse me, but could you speak a bit more slowly?
I couldn't catch what you said.

對不起，你可否說慢一點？我聽不懂你說的。

外國人：Oh, I'm sorry. Do you remember Mr. Baker?

喔，抱歉。你記得貝克爾先生嗎？

中國人：Yes, of course. 是的，當然。

外國人：I met you at Mr. Baker's house.

我在貝克爾先生家見過你。

HINT BANK————————————

- *a bit* 一點點

＊ 在不確定對方是否是某人時，用" You're～，aren't you？"的句型來詢問，而
且語尾的聲調要往上揚。

中國人： Yes, I remember now.
　　　　是的，現在我記起來了。

外國人： It was about one year ago, wasn't it?
　　　　大約是一年前，不是嗎？

中國人： Yes, I believe it was. 是的，我想是的。

外國人： You're looking great. You've *lost some weight*, haven't
　　　　you? 你看起來好極了，你瘦了些，不是嗎？

中國人： What does "lost weight" mean?
　　　　"lost weight"是什麼意思？

外國人： "Lose weight" means to become thinner, not to be as
　　　　heavy as you were.
　　　　"lost weight"是指變瘦，不像你以前那麼重。

中國人： I see. Yes. I stopped smoking and began to exercise.
　　　　我明白了，是的，我停止抽煙而且開始運動。

外國人： I admire you. How do you exercise? Do you jog?
　　　　我很欽佩你，你是怎麼運動的？你慢跑嗎？

中國人： I beg your pardon? 對不起，請再說一次。

外國人： Jog. It means to run a long distance at a slow and
　　　　steady pace.
　　　　慢跑，它是指以緩慢、規則的步伐，跑一段長距離。

HINT BANK————————————

- *lose weight* 體重減少；變瘦（相反詞是 *gain weight*）
- jog〔dʒɑg〕*v.* 慢跑；緩慢平穩地進行

中國人：Oh, yes. I didn't understand your pronunciation. Yes,
　　　　I'm a jogger. I do 10 kilometers a day.
　　　　喔，是的，我不懂你的發音。是的，我慢跑，每天跑十
　　　　公里。

外國人：No wonder you look *in great shape*.
　　　　難怪你看起來身體情況很好。

中國人：I think stopping smoking was the smartest thing I
　　　　ever did. 我想，停止抽煙是我所做過最聰明的事。

外國人：Most people gain weight when they stop smoking.
　　　　Didn't you?
　　　　大部分人停止抽煙時，體重會增加，你會這樣嗎？

中國人：At first. But when I started jogging I lost it.
　　　　剛開始的時候，不過我開始慢跑以後體重就減少了。

HINT BANK───────────────

・pronunciation〔prə͵nʌnsɪˈeʃən〕*n.* 發音（注意這個字很容易拼錯）

＊" in great shape "表示「身體狀況很好」。

⟱ Grammar and Usage ⟰

1. 附加問句

在會話中，常用「附加問句」來表示叮嚀，或是詢問對方的意向，有時也用「附加問句」，使所說的話更委婉。在使用附加問句時，有二點必須注意的：

(1) 附加問句的動詞

如果主要子句的動詞是肯定，則附加疑問的動詞要爲否定。若主要子句的動詞是否定，則附加疑問的動詞要爲肯定。而附加疑問的動詞，必須和主要子句的動詞時態一致。例：

- You're Mr. Lee, *aren't you*? （你是李先生，不是嗎？）
- You didn't understand, *did you*? （你不懂，對吧？）
- You've lost some weight, *haven't you*?
  （你體重減輕了，不是嗎？）

另外，主要子句如果是一般動詞，附加問句的動詞則用 "do"。例：

- You remember Mr. Lin, *don't you*?
  （你記得林先生，不是嗎？）
- He told you the story, *didn't he*?
  （他告訴你這故事，不是嗎？）

2. 附加問句的音調

附加問句的語尾有上升和下降二種情形。例：

- It's a fine day ↘, isn't it ↘? （今天天氣很好，不是嗎？）

這句話的語尾下降，只是單純地使話更委婉，或有叮嚀的意思。

- You've been to Hsitou ↘, haven't you ↗?（你去過溪頭，不是嗎？）這句話的語尾上揚，含有「詢問、質問」的意味。

◣ First Week, Sixth Day ◢

How to Answer Questions

── 第一週，第六天　如何回答問題 ──

◖ **BASIC DIALOGUES** ◗

1. A : *Are you from* the United States？
　　　 你是美國人嗎？（你來自美國嗎？）

　 B : Yes, I am. 是的，我是。

2. A : Do you plan to stay here long？你計劃在這裏停留很久嗎？

　 B : No, I don't. I'm leaving Taiwan next month.
　　　 不，下個月我要離開台灣。

3. A : Have you traveled much in Taiwan？
　　　 你有沒有常常到台灣各地去旅遊？

　 B : No, I haven't. I have only visited Sun Moon Lake and
　　　 the National Palace Museum.
　　　 沒有，我祇到過日月潭和故宮博物院。

4. A : *You've been to* many countries, haven't you？
　　　 你去過許多國家，不是嗎？

B：Yes, I've been to Germany, France, Spain, India and England. 是的，我去過德國、法國、西班牙、印度以及英國。

5. A：Can I reserve a seat to Kaohsiung? 我可以預訂一個到高雄的座位嗎？

B：Yes, you can. 是的，可以。

6. A：Does the plane leave from the Chiang Kai-shek International Airport or from the Kaohsiung International Airport? 飛機是從中正國際機場，還是從高雄國際機場起飛？

B：It leaves from the Chiang Kai-shek International Airport. 是從中正國際機場起飛的。

7. A：Would you like to take the 9:00 or 10:00 flight? 你想搭九點還是十點的班機？

B：*Either will do.* 兩班都可以。

8. A：Where do you live? 你住在哪裏？

B：I live in New York. 我住在紐約。

9. A：When does the train arrive in Taichung? 火車什麼時候抵達台中？

B：I believe it arrives in Taichung at 12:30. 我想是在十二點半抵達。

10. A：*How do you like* staying in Taiwan? 你覺得停留在台灣如何？

B：I like it very much. How about you? 我非常喜歡，你呢？

HINT BANK ─────────────

・reserve〔rɪ'zɜv〕*v*. 預定（車座、戲座等）。

＊問別人出生地、籍貫的句型是 " Are you from～ ？"
＊問別人「覺得如何？」、「覺得怎樣？」的句型是 " How do you like～ ？"

◀ APPLIED CONVERSATION ▶ 在火車上與外國人聊天
Speaking to a Foreigner on a Train

中國人： ***May I introduce myself***? My
name is John Wang.
請容我自我介紹，我叫王約翰。

外國人： How do you do, Mr. Wang.
My name is Brown…George
Brown.
王先生，你好（幸會）。
我叫布朗…喬治・布朗。

中國人： I'm very happy to meet you. Are you going through
to Taichung. 幸會。你是直達台中嗎？

外國人： Yes. ***How about yourself***? 是的，你呢？

中國人： Yes, I'm going to Taichung, too. Is this your first
trip to Taichung?
是的，我也是要去台中。這是你第一次到台中旅行嗎？

外國人： Oh, no, I've been to Taichung many times.
喔，不是，我去過台中很多次。

中國人： Are you engaged in business here in Taiwan?
你是在台灣做生意嗎？

HINT BANK————————————

• ***go through to*** 直達　　 trip〔trɪp〕*n*.（特指短程的）旅行
• ***be engaged in*** 從事於

* 在自我介紹時，常用的句型是 "May I introduce myself？"

外國人： Yes, I'm with an import-export firm. We have branch
offices in Taipei.

是的，我在一家進出口公司工作。我們公司在台北有分公司。

中國人： I see. Do you have your family with you?

我明白了。你的家人是不是跟你在一起？

外國人： Yes, my wife and my youngest daughter are here in
Taipei with me, but my son and another daughter are
attending college in the United States.

是的，我太太以及最小的女兒都和我在台北這裏，不過我
的兒子和另外一個女兒在美國上大學。

中國人： I have two sons and a daughter. My eldest boy entered
National Taiwan University this year. My daughter is
still in high school.

我有兩個兒子、一個女兒。我最大的兒子今年進台大，女
兒還在唸高中。

外國人： *Are you in business*？你是做生意的嗎？

中國人： Yes, I'm in the advertising business.

是的，我是做廣告業的。

外國人： Well, I'm sure it must be quite interesting.

嗯，我相信那一定非常有趣。

中國人： Yes, it is. 是的，是很有趣。

HINT BANK

* *in business* 做生意

* "I'm with an import-export firm."句中用 "be with"是表示「在～上班」
的意思。"an import-export firm"是「進出口公司」即指「貿易公司」。

外國人： If you are staying in Taichung, why don't we have lunch together this week?

如果你要待在台中的話，我們何不在這個星期一塊兒吃午飯呢？

中國人： Well, that's very kind of you, but I don't think I shall have any time before Thursday.

嗯，你真好（謝謝你的親切）。不過，我想在星期四以前，我不會有時間的。

外國人： Thursday would be fine for me. ***Shall we say*** 12：30 at the Hotel New Taichung?

星期四對我來說太好了。我們十二點半在新台中飯店如何？

中國人： Wonderful. I'll wait for you in the hotel lobby.

好極了，我會在飯店大廳等你。

外國人： You speak English very well. Have you ever been to the United States?

你英文講得很好。你曾經去過美國嗎？

中國人： Only once, when I was quite young. I spent one year studying in Seattle.

只去過一次，那時候我還很小。我在西雅圖讀了一年書。

外國人： And you've never been back since?

從那以後，你就從不曾回去過了嗎？

HINT BANK ─────────────────

• lobby〔'lɑbɪ〕*n.*（飯店、戲院的）大廳；休息室

＊ "Why don't we～?"「我們何不～？」是勸誘、邀請的用語。

＊ "Shall we say～?"「～如何？」是表示提議的用語。

中國人： No, unfortunately. 令人遺憾的是，不曾。

外國人： Well, anyway, you and your wife must visit us when we return to Taipei. We live in Shihlin. Here is my card. You can *get in touch with* me at my office.

　　　　嗯，無論如何，我們回台北時，你和你太太一定要來看我們。我們住在士林。這裏是我的名片，你可以在我的辦公室聯絡到我。

中國人： Thank you. 謝謝你。

HINT BANK

· *get in touch with* 和～聯絡；和～接觸

* "You and your wife must visit us." 用 "must" 是表示「請務必」的意思。
* 「名片」是用 "my card" 而不是 "name card"。

基本用法表達

2nd Week　Basic Forms of Explanation

▌Second Week, First Day▐

How to Explain Places and Locations

第二週・第一天　如何說明地點和場所

▌BASIC DIALOGUES▐

1. A : Where's my umbrella? 我的雨傘在哪裏？

　B : It's in the umbrella stand at the entrance.
　　　　在入口處的雨傘架裏。

2. A : I'm afraid I've lost my cigarette lighter.
　　　　恐怕我的打火機丢掉了。

　B : I think I saw it on the sofa behind the table *a few minutes ago.*
　　　　我想，幾分鐘前我在那張桌子後面的沙發上看到過。

3. A : Where can I find the foreign book section?
　　　　我在哪裏可以找到外國書的部門？

　B : You can find it to your right as you go down this aisle.
　　　　你沿這個通道往下走的時候，可以在你的右手邊找到。

4. A：**What floor is** Mr. Wilson's office **on**?
　　威爾遜先生的辦公室在幾樓？

　　B：It's on the fourth. 在四樓。

5. A：Do you know where I can find the rest room?
　　你知道在哪裏可以找到休息室？

　　B：You'll find it down the corridor on your right.
　　你沿著走廊走下去，在你的右手邊就可以找得到。

6. A：Which way is the editorial department?
　　編輯部在哪個方向？

　　B：It's down the hall to the left, sir.
　　先生，在沿這個大廳下去的左邊。

7. A：Where did you meet him? 你在哪裏遇見他？

　　B：I met him as I was walking down Hsimenting Street
　　near Far East Department Store.
　　當我走在靠近遠東百貨公司的西門町街上時，就遇見他了。

8. A：**Where shall I meet you**? 我要在哪裏和你見面？

　　B：I'll be waiting for you in the lobby of the President
　　Hotel. 我會在統一飯店的大廳等你。

HINT BANK───────────

- stand〔stænd〕*n.* 架；台
- lighter〔'laɪtə〕*n.* 打火機（= *cigarette lighter*）
- **rest room**〔美〕（商店、戲院等的）洗手間；廁所；（設有洗手間的）休息室
- corridor〔'kɔrədə〕*n.* 走廊

* 問「在幾樓？」的句型是 "What floor is～on？"。注意不要漏掉 "on"。
* "I met him as I was walking down...." 句中的 "as" 是指「正當～的時候」。

9. A： Is the bus stop for Shihlin near here?

到士林的公車站是不是在這兒附近？

B： Yes, it's just around the corner.

是的，就在附近。

10. A： Can I park my car *in front of* your office?

我可否將車子停在你們辦公室前面？

B： I think you can. 我想你可以。

HINT BANK———————————————

• *around the corner* 在附近；在轉角處

＊ " the bus stop for ～ " 是指「往～的公車站」。

⋈ APPLIED CONVERSATION ⋈ 警察指路

A Policeman Showing the Way

外國人： Excuse me, I wonder if you could *give me a few directions*. 對不起，你是否能給我一些指示。

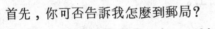

警　察： I'll be glad to if I can. 我很樂意，如果我能的話。

外國人： First, can you tell me how to get to the post office? 首先，你可否告訴我怎麼到郵局？

警　察： Certainly. It's straight down this street. Just keep walking for about 200 meters. You'll see it on your right. 可以。它就在沿著這條街直走下去。大約只要一直走兩百公尺，你會看到它在你的右手邊。

外國人： Thank you. And now, will you tell me how to find the National Theatre? 謝謝你，那麼，請你告訴我怎麼到國家劇院？

警　察： The National Theatre is *within walking distance* too — it's about a 10-minute walk. 國家劇院也是在走得到的範圍內。——大約是十分鐘。

HINT BANK————————————————————

・ *and now* 那麼；且　　*within walking distance* 在走得到的範圍內

＊ 詢問別人時，較有禮貌的問法是 " I wonder if you could～? "

＊ "direction" 是「指示」的意思。"give direction" 含有「指點道路或指示方法」的意思。

外國人：***Which way is it***？哪一個方向？

警　察：Go down this street and turn right at the second inter-section. You'll come to a large office building on your right. The theater is next to it on the right.
　　　　沿著這條街走下去，在第二個十字路口右轉。你會看到一棟很大的辦公大樓在你的右手邊。劇院在這棟大樓右邊隔壁。

外國人：Is the Public Library in this area？
　　　　公立圖書館是不是在這個地區？

警　察：The Library is quite a distance from here. If you don't have a car, you'd better take the bus.
　　　　圖書館離這裏有一段相當的距離，如果你沒有車的話，最好是搭巴士。

外國人：***Which bus do I take***？我搭哪一路巴士？

警　察：Take the bus for the railroad station. I think it's No. 36. The bus stop's just in front of the Library.
　　　　搭往火車站的巴士，我想是三十六路吧。公車站就在（公立）圖書館的前面。

外國人：Is there a bus stop near here？這附近有沒有巴士站？

警　察：Yes, there's one right across the street.
　　　　有的，對街就有一個。

外國人：One last question — can you recommend a good depart-ment store？最後一個問題——你能推薦一家好百貨公司給我嗎？

HINT BANK─────────────────────

* intersection〔͵ɪntɚˈsɛkʃən〕*n.* 十字路口　　　***come to*** 來到；成為

* "right across the street" 句中的 "right" 和 "just" 的意思相同，都是指「正好；剛好」的意思。

警　察： Well, there are two — the Pacific Department Store
and the Tonlin Department Store.
嗯，有兩家——太平洋百貨公司跟統領百貨公司。

外國人： Which one is larger？哪一家比較大？

警　察： I believe the Pacific Department Store is larger.
我想太平洋百貨公司比較大。

外國人： Is it very far from here？離這裏很遠嗎？

警　察： Well, it's too far to walk. You can take the bus.
嗯，太遠了，沒辦法走路去。你可以搭公車。

外國人： Is the bus station close by？公車車站近不近？

警　察： Yes, it's about a block down the street. If you take
the bus, get off at the fourth stop. You'll see the
department store when you get off the the bus.
是的，大約在沿這條街下去的一個街區。如果你搭公車的
話，在第四站下車。當你一下公車時，就會看到百貨公司。

外國人： Well, you've been most kind. Thank you so much.
嗯，你真好，非常謝謝你。

警　察： Not at all. I'm glad I was able to help you.
不客氣，我很高興能幫你忙。

HINT BANK

- block〔blɑk〕*n.*（美）市街的一區

* " close by " 是「在…旁邊」也可以用 " near by "。

Second Week, Second Day

How to Express Time and Dates

第二週，第二天　如何說明時間和日期

BASIC DIALOGUES

1. A: What time is it, please? 請問，現在幾點？
   B: It's half past nine. 九點半。

2. A: *Do you have the time*, please? 請問現在幾點？
   B: It's 7:35. 七點三十五分。

3. A: I'll see you at seven sharp. 七點正見。
   B: Okay. I'll be waiting. 好的，我會等你。

4. A: At what time will you be at the station?
      你幾點會在車站？
   B: I'll be at the station at 6:15. 我六點十五分會在車站。

5. A: At what time does the program begin? 節目什麼時候開始？
   B: It begins at eight forty-five. 八點四十五分開始。

6. A: ***When will you be back***? 你什麼時候會回來？

　B: I'll be back by ten thirty. 我十點半之前會回來。

7. A: What day is today? 今天星期幾？

　B: Today is Tuesday. 今天是星期二。

8. A: ***What's today's date***? 今天是幾號？

　B: Today is the 15th of May. 今天是五月十五日。

9. A　When will the meeting be held?

　　會議什麼時候舉行？

　B: It will be held on Wednesday the 21st. It's a week from this coming Wednesday.

　　會議是二十一日星期三舉行，離這一個星期三還有一個星期。

10. A: Did you meet him yesterday? 昨天你見過他嗎？

　B: No. I met him the day before yesterday.

　　不，前天我見過他。

11. A: When will Mary be coming? 瑪麗什麼時候來？

　B: She'll be coming the day after tomorrow. 她後天來。

HINK BANK ─────────────

- program〔'progræm〕*n.* 節目；計劃（表）；預定（表）
- coming〔'kʌmɪŋ〕*adj.* 其次的　　***the day before yesterday*** 前天
- ***the day after tomorrow*** 後天

* 問別人「現在幾點？」除了用 "What time is it?" 之外，還可以用 "Do you have the time?"
* " by ten thirty " 用 " by " 是指「在十點半之前」。

12. **A**：Did you read Mr. Wilson's new book?

　　　你讀過威爾遜先生的新書嗎？

　　B：Yes, I read it *a couple of weeks ago*.

　　　是的，我幾個星期前讀過。

13. **A**：How long are you planning to stay in Taiwan?

　　　你計劃在台灣停留多久？

　　B：I'm planning to stay in Taiwan for three months.

　　　我計劃在台灣停留三個月。

HINT BANK────────────────────────────

・ *a couple of* 〔美口〕數個；幾個

＊" for three months "用" for "是表示「持續三個月期間」。

◀ APPLIED CONVERSATION ▶　計劃週末

Planning for the Weekend

外國人：Hello, Mei-mei. 嗨，美美。

中國人：Hello, Susan. *Come on in.*
　　　　嗨，蘇珊，請進。

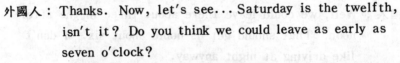

外國人：Thank you. I came to talk
　　　　over our plans for our picnic
　　　　this coming weekend.
　　　　謝謝你，我來討論我們下個週
　　　　末野餐的計劃。

中國人：That's a good idea. Please
　　　　sit down. 好主意，請坐下。

外國人：Thanks. Now, let's see... Saturday is the twelfth,
　　　　isn't it? Do you think we could leave as early as
　　　　seven o'clock?
　　　　謝謝。嗯，讓我想想看…星期六是十二號，不是嗎？你
　　　　想我們可以早在七點鐘就離開嗎？

中國人：Of course, the earlier the better. *If we could leave
　　　　even half an hour earlier*, we could avoid the morning
　　　　traffic. 當然，愈早愈好。如果我們甚至能提早半個鐘頭離
　　　　開，就會避免早上的交通尖峯時間。

HINT BANK ─────────────

- *talk over* 商議；討論　　*let's see* 讓我想想看（ = *let me see* ）

* "Come on in." 用" on "是表示強調。

* "We could leave～." 用過去式的" could "是表示「也許很勉強，但是可以的
　話…。」的語氣。

外國人：My! That's awfully early, isn't it?

哎呀！那可眞早，不是嗎？

中國人：Well, we'd have to get up at least an hour earlier. But that wouldn't be too bad. We could get everything ready the night before.

嗯，我們至少必須提早一個鐘頭起床。不過那並不會太糟。我們在前一晚就可以把所有的東西都準備好。

外國人：Yes, I suppose so. Look, I'll come over Friday evening and help you prepare the sandwiches and other things that we'll take.

是的，我想是的。喂，我星期五晚上過來，幫你準備三明治，及其他我們要帶的東西。

中國人：Oh, that'll be fine. 喔，那太好了。

外國人：And what about the trip back? 那麼回程呢？

中國人：Well, we could leave there about three in the afternoon. That should get us home about six. I don't like driving at night anyway.

嗯，我們可以在下午三點左右離開那裏。這樣我們六點左右就應該到家了。無論如何，我不喜歡晚上開車。

外國人：How about having dinner at my house after we get back? 我們回來以後，在我家吃晚飯如何？

中國人：*That would be wonderful*. 那太棒了。

HINT BANK————————————

- *get ready* 預備；準備
- *look*！（作感歎詞用，用以引起對方注意）喂；瞧；你看；小心

* "That would be wonderful." 用 "would" 是表示「如果能那樣的話」的語氣。

外國人：All right, I'll ask Mother to have dinner ready for us
about seven. That should give us time to get washed
up. 好的，我會要媽媽在七點左右，就幫我們把晚餐準備好，
那應該會給我們時間洗好手臉。

中國人：Now that everything is settled. I'm sure we'll have
a great weekend.
既然一切都解決了，我確信我們會有一個很棒的周末。

外國人：Yes, of course. By the way, what time is it now?
是的，當然。順便一提，現在幾點？

中國人：It's twenty-five minutes after three. 三點二十五分。

外國人：*I've got to go now.* I have an appointment at four.
我現在要走了，四點有約會。

中國人：Well, then, I'll be waiting for you Friday evening.
嗯，那麼，星期五晚上我等你。

HINT BANK─────────────

- *wash up* 飯前洗臉洗手；洗餐具；做餐後收拾工作
- *now that* 既然（ = since ）

＊“ get washed up ”用“ get ”是含有「完成～」的意思。

Second Week, Third Day

How to Express Quantity and Volume

第二週，第三天　如何說明數量與容量

BASIC DIALOGUES

1. **A :** May I help you, sir? 先生，有什麼可以效勞的？

   B : I'd like to buy a pair of gloves. 我想買一雙手套。

2. **A :** *How many* pairs of shoes do you have? 你有幾雙鞋？

   B : I have three; *one* is brown and *the others* are black.
   我有三雙，一雙是棕色的，其它（兩雙）是黑色的

3. **A :** Will you give me ten 1-dollar and five 5-dollar stamps?
   請你給我十張一塊錢，及五張五塊錢的郵票，好嗎？

   B : Yes, sir. 好的

4. **A :** Could you change this thousand dollar note into nine one-
   hundred dollar bills and ten ten-dollar coins?

   可否請你將這張一千元的鈔票，換成九張一百元的鈔票，及
   十個十元的硬幣？

   B : I'm sorry, but I don't have any one-hundred dollar bills
   with me. 抱歉，可是我身上沒有任何一百元的鈔票。

5. A : How many hours does it take to go to New York by
train？搭火車到紐約要花幾個鐘頭？

B : It will take about four hours by superexpress train.
搭超級特快車的話，大約要花四個鐘頭。

6. A : *How much* sugar would you like in your tea？
你的茶要加多少糖？

B : A couple of spoonfuls will be plenty, thank you.
幾湯匙就夠多了，謝謝你。

7. A : *How long* do you think the bridge is？你想這橋有多長？

B : It's about 200 meters long. 大約有兩百公尺長。

8. A : How many pounds do you weigh？你的體重是幾磅？

B : I think I weigh about 135 pounds.
我想是一百三十五磅左右。

A : Then, I outweigh you by 20 pounds. 那麼，我比你重二十磅。

9. A : What can I do for you today？今天有什麼我可以效勞的？

B : I'd like to have a dozen eggs. 我想要一打蛋。

HINT BANT

- note〔not〕*n.*〔英〕紙幣；鈔票（＝〔美〕*bill*）
- outweigh〔aut'we〕*v.* 比～重；重於

* 詢問對方「有什麼事？」的句型有："May I help you？"，"What can I do for you？"，"Can I help you？"等等。店員或餐館的服務人員常用這些句來招呼客人。但是，在其他場合也可使用。

* "will be plenty"是表示「夠了」，"plenty"和"enough"的意思一樣。但是，在會話上較常用"plenty"。

* "I outweigh you by～."句中的"by"是指二者比較之下，其間差距。

◀ APPLIED CONVERSATION ▶ 寄信到美國

Sending a letter to the United States

比　爾：Say, Tom, what's the airmail
postage to the United States?
喂，湯姆，寄到美國的航空郵
件的郵資是多少？

中國人：It's 16 dollars. That's the
minimum. It's higher if the
letter is heavier than *a certain number of* grams.
十六元。這是最低的金額。如
果信件超過一定的重量，花費
就更高。

比　爾：What's the domestic postage？ 國內的郵資是多少？

中國人：It's 3 dollars for letters and 1.5 dollars for post
cards. 信三元，明信片一塊半。

比　爾：I guess this letter will go for 16 dollars.
我想這封信要十六元（的郵資）。

中國人：Did you write to your mother？ 你寫給你媽媽嗎？

HINT BANK───────────────

· postage〔ˋpostɪdʒ〕n. 郵資　minimum〔ˋmɪnəməm〕n. 最低額；最低限度
· *go for* 適用於；應用於　domestic〔dəˋmɛstɪk〕adj. 屬於本國的

＊ " a certain " 是用來表示「確定的；（某）一定的」，例：" at a certain
hour "（在一定的時間）， " at a certain place "（在一定的地點）。

比　爾： Yes, the last time I wrote to her I told her I'd gained 20 pounds during my six months in Taiwan. She
was quite worried.

是的，上次我寫信給她，告訴她我在台灣這半年增加了二十
磅的體重。她相當擔心。

中國人： *Have you lost any weight* since you wrote to your mother the last time?

從你上次寫信給你媽媽以後，你的體重減輕了嗎？

比　爾： Well, I haven't lost any, but I haven't gained any
either. 嗯，我沒有減輕，不過也沒有增加。

中國人： How much do you weigh? 你的體重是多少？

比　爾： I think I weigh about 170 pounds. One hundred and
fifty *would be about right for me.*

我想大約是一百七十磅左右。一百五十對我來說，應該是
差不多剛剛好。

中國人： Incidentally, how tall are you? 順便問一下，你多高？

比　爾： I'm five feet nine inches. How tall are you?

我是五呎九吋高。你多高？

中國人： Oh, I'm only five feet six. 喔，我只有五呎六吋。

HINT BANK─────────────────────

· incidentally 〔͵ɪnsə'dɛntḷɪ〕 *adv.* 順便（說）；附帶地

＊ " I'd gained 20 pounds." 在書信中應該是用 " I've gained ～." 但是，在間
接敘述法中，主要子句若是過去式，就要用過去完成式來敘述，所以用" I'd "。

＊ " ～ would be about right for me " 用 " would " 是表示假設語氣。" about
right " 是指「差不多剛剛好」。

比　爾：You look taller than that. 你看起來比五呎六吋高。

中國人：Say, Bill, ***how about going out*** ? I want to buy a few things. 喂，比爾，出去如何？我想買一些東西。

比　爾：Sure. What are you going to buy？
　　　當然，你打算買什麼？

中國人：Well, I want to buy a couple of pencils and a bottle of ink. If we have time I'd like to buy a pair of gloves, too. 嗯，我想買幾隻鉛筆和一瓶墨水。如果我們有時間的話，我也想買一雙手套。

媽　媽：Oh, Tom, if you're going out I wish you'd buy some things for me.
　　　喔，湯姆，如果你要出去的話，我希望你替我買些東西。

中國人：Yes, Mother. ***What do you want me to get*** ?
　　　是的，媽，你要我買什麼？

媽　媽：Let me see... Oh, yes, a dozen eggs, a pound of butter, a jar of jam and a loaf of bread.
　　　讓我想想看…喔，是的，一打蛋、一磅奶油、一瓶果醬以及一條麵包。

中國人：***Is that all*** ? 就這些嗎？

HINT BANK————————————————

* " I wish you'd ～. "是表示「希望對方做～。」是請求、拜託別人的句子。

* " Is that all ? "是表示「就這些嗎？」或「這樣就夠嗎？」

媽　媽：Yes, I think so... Oh, yes, if you see some nice grapes
　　　　at the fruit store, buy a couple of bunches.
　　　　是的，我想是的…喔，是的，如果你看到水果店有些不錯的
　　　　葡萄的話，買幾串回來。

中國人：Will you give me some money, Mother ?
　　　　媽，你給我些錢好嗎？

媽　媽：Of course. Here's five hundred dollars. That should
　　　　be enough. 當然，這是五百元，應該夠了。

中國人：Let's go, Bill. 我們走吧，比爾。

HINT BANK

・bunch〔bʌntʃ〕*n.*（香蕉、葡萄等的）串；束

▌Second Week, Fourth Day▐

How to Express Degree or Level

第二週・第四天　如何說明程度

▌ BASIC DIALOGUES ▐

1. **A**：Do you like apples？你喜歡蘋果嗎？

   B：Yes, very much. 是的，非常喜歡。

2. **A**：Are you tired? 你累了嗎？

   B：No, *not in the least*. 不，一點也不累。

3. **A**：Nobody can sing better than Betty.

   　　沒有人比貝蒂唱得更好。

   B：I think you're right. 我想，你是對的。

4. **A**：Who is the most brilliant student in your class？

   　　誰是你們班上最出色的學生？

   B：Well, there are many excellent students, but I think John is the best.

   　　嗯，有很多學生都很優秀，不過我想約翰是最好的。

5. **A**：How was Miss Stone's performance？

   　　史東小姐的演出如何？

B : Her acting was just ordinary, but Miss Morrison's was a brilliant performance.
她的演技很平常，不過莫莉遜小姐的演出很出色。

6. A : Mary won the championship at the tennis tournament.
瑪莉在網球比賽中獲得冠軍。

B : *I don't wonder.* Not many girls can play tennis as well as she can. 我不會感到詫異，女孩子中並沒有很多打網球打得像她那麼好。

7. A : *Do you follow me*? 你聽得懂我說的嗎？

B : I'm afraid not. Won't you please speak a little more slowly? 恐怕沒有，麻煩你說慢一點好嗎？

8. A : Don't walk so fast. We still have plenty of time.
別走這麼快，我們還有很多時間。

B : Really? It's already 4:25 by my watch.
眞的嗎？我的錶已經四點二十五分了。

A : I think your watch is 10 minutes fast. My watch says 4:15. 我想，你的錶快了十分鐘。我的錶是四點十五分。

HINT BANK ─────────────────

· *not in the least* 一點也不（= *not at all*）
· brilliant〔'brɪljənt〕*adj.* 出色的　　performance〔pə'fɔrməns〕*n.* 演出；表演
· tournament〔'tɜnəmənt〕*n.* 比賽　　championship〔'tʃæmpɪən‚ʃɪp〕*n.* 冠軍
· follow〔'fɑlo〕*v.* 聽得懂；了解

* "We still have plenty of time." 句中的 " still " 可以用 " yet " 來替換，所以，也可以說成："We have plenty of time yet."。要注意的是，" still " 是放在動詞之前或 be 動詞之後。而 " yet " 則應放在句尾。

* 表示「鐘錶的快慢」是用 " fast " 和 " slow "，如：" 10 minutes fast "（快十分鐘），" 10 minutes slow "（慢十分鐘）。

⟫⟨ APPLIED CONVERSATION ⟩⟫ 談棒球
Talking about Baseball

中國人： Well, John, the baseball sea-
son is coming around again.

嗯，約翰，棒球季又來臨了。

外國人： I've already got a ticket for
the opening game.

我已經拿到第一場比賽的票。

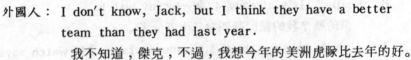

中國人： That's wonderful. By the
way, John, *what do you think
of* the Jaguars this year?

太棒了。順便一提，約翰，你
覺得今年美洲虎隊如何？

外國人： I don't know, Jack, but I think they have a better
team than they had last year.

我不知道，傑克，不過，我想今年的美洲虎隊比去年的好。

中國人： Why do you think that? 你爲什麼會那樣想？

外國人： *For one thing*, they have the best infield in the entire
league. They've got a brilliant combination in Tom at
third and William at short stop.

HINT BANK

- *come around* （季節等）再來臨　opening〔ˈopənɪŋ, ˈopnɪŋ〕*adj.* 第一次
- jaguar〔ˈdʒægwɑr〕*n.* 〔動〕美洲虎
- *for one thing* 首先，一則（用在申述理由時用之）
- infield〔ˈɪn͵fild〕*n.* 內野手　league〔lig〕*n.* （棒球等的）比賽聯盟
- third〔ˈθɝd〕*n.* 三壘（= *third base*）　　*short stop*〔棒球〕游擊手

　　　一則，他們有全部比賽聯盟中，最好的內野手。他們有三壘手湯姆，和游擊手威廉出色的組合。

中國人：Yes, I guess you're right. 是的，我想你是對的。

外國人：Their pitching staff is still a bit weak, I think, **but far better than last year**, and they have some powerful batters, especially Johnny.

　　　我想，他們的投手群還是有點弱，不過，比去年好得多了，而且他們有些強打者，特別是強尼。

中國人：He hit .361 last year, didn't he?
　　　他去年的打擊率是三成六一，不是嗎？

外國人：Yes, with 35 home runs. He's really a power hitter.
　　　是的，有三十五支全壘打，他真是一個強打者。

中國人：What do you think of the Jaguars' new manager?
　　　你覺得美洲虎隊的新經理如何？

外國人：Well, Thomas certainly knows baseball and he's a wizard **when it comes to handling players**. He has the confidence of every man on the team.

　　　嗯，湯瑪斯的確懂棒球，而且到了要指揮球員時，他是個行家。他獲得球隊裏每一個人的信任。

HINT BANK───────────────

- pitching〔'pɪtʃɪŋ〕*n.*〔棒球〕投球　　batter〔'bætɚ〕*n.* 打擊手
- **home run**〔棒球〕全壘打　　wizard〔'wɪzəd〕*n.* 行家；專家（＝*expert*）

＊".361" 唸作 "three-sixty-one" 這是打擊率的表示方法。

＊"power hitter" 是指「強打者」，也可以用 "powerful hitter"。

中國人 : He was an active player for a long time before he
　　　　became manager, wasn't he?
　　　　在成爲經理前，有很長一段時間，他是個活躍的棒球球
　　　　員，不是嗎？

外國人 : Yes, he was one of the most brilliant first basemen
　　　　in the history of professional baseball in the U.S.A.
　　　　是的，他是美國職業棒球史上，最出色的一壘手之一。

中國人 : Well, I certainly hope they win the pennant again this
　　　　year. 嗯，我眞的很希望他們今年再度贏得錦標。

外國人 : I do, too. 我也是。

HINT BANK────────────────

・pennant〔'pɛnənt〕*n.* 〔美〕錦標

Grammar and Usage

1. 表示「非常；很」的字

通常我們用 " very（much）", " so ", " too " 來表示「非常；很」的意思。

- The sky is *very* clear.（天空非常晴朗。）
- I'm *so* sad to hear the news.（聽到這消息，我非常的悲傷。）
- It's *too* hot to stay at home.
  （天氣太熱，以致無法待在家裏。）

除了以上的字彙之外，在會話中常用 "*awfully*", "*terribly*", "*tremendously*" 來表達「非常；很」的意思。

2. 表示「一點也不」的用法

"（not）in the least", "（not）at all", "in the slightest degree" 都是用在否定句中，表示「一點也不～」的意思。

- I *can't* believe him *at all*.（我一點也不能相信他。）
- He was *not in the least hurt*.（他一點也沒受傷。）

除了用這幾個用法之外，也可以用 "nothing"，例：

- I knew *nothing* of it.（我一點也不知道。）

3. 比較的用法

表示比較時，通常是在形容詞之後，加 "-er" 或 "-est"。但是，如果有二個音節以上的形容詞，如：" important ", " interesting "，則應在前加 "more", "most" 形成比較級、最高級。還有一些不規則變化的形容詞，如：" good ", " well ", " many ", " much ", " little " 等，這些字的比較級和最高級，必須熟記後，才會使用。

Second Week, Fifth Day

How to Explain Causes and Reasons

第二週，第五天　如何說明原因與理由

BASIC DIALOGUES

1. A： Why didn't you go to Betty's house yesterday?
為什麼你昨天沒去貝蒂家？
B： Because I had a slight cold. 因為我有點輕微的感冒。
A： That's too bad. Are you all right now?
那眞不幸，你現在好了嗎？
B： Yes, thanks. 是的，謝謝。

2. A： Do you know why he failed? 你知道他為什麼失敗？
B： I think his failure was due to his carelessness.
我想他失敗是由於粗心。

3. A： ***Can you explain the reason why it happened***?
你可否解釋這為什麼會發生？
B： It happened because they were all careless.
這會發生是因為他們都太不小心了。

4. A：What made him do such a thing, I wonder？
　　　我在想，是什麼令他做出這種事來？

　B：The reason is simple enough. 理由簡單之至。

5. A：How is it that you didn't apply for the position？
　　　你怎麼會沒有申請那個職位？

　B：There was no particular reason. 沒有特殊的理由。

6. A：The accident happened because he was speeding.
　　　這個意外會發生，是因為他超速駕駛。

　B：You're right. It wouldn't have happened if he hadn't
　　　been speeding.
　　　你說得對，如果他沒有超速駕駛的話，就不會發生意外了。

7. A：*Who was to blame for the accident*？這個意外應歸咎於誰？

　B：I suppose it was the man on the bicycle
　　　我想是那個騎腳踏車的人。

8. A：We are going to the movies. Will you join us？
　　　我們要去看電影，你要跟我們一道去嗎？

　B：I'm very sorry, but I can't. 很抱歉，我不能去。

　A：Why not？為什麼不？

　B：Because I have some business to attend to now.
　　　因為，我現在有些事要料理。

HINT BANK─────────────

　• *be due to* 由於　　　speed〔spid〕v. 超速駕駛
　• *be to blame* 應受譴責；應負責任

　＊ 在聽到不好的事或消息，而表示遺憾的說法是 "That's too bad."（那真不幸。）
　＊ "It wouldn't have～if he hadn't～." 這是表示「和過去事實相反」的假設法。

❌ APPLIED CONVERSATION ❌ 探望生病的朋友

Meeting a Sick Friend

中國人： Hello, Caroline. ***How are you feeling***? 嗨，卡洛琳，你現在覺得怎麼樣？

外國人： Much better, Tina. Thanks for coming to see me. 好多了，婷娜，謝謝你來看我。

中國人： It was such a shock to hear that you were in an accident. How did it happen? 聽到你出了意外，真是很大的震驚。是怎麼發生的？

外國人： It all happened so quickly I really don't know who was in the wrong. 發生得太快了，以至於我真的不知道誰不對。

中國人： Were you driving the car? 是你開車嗎？

外國人： No, Fred was driving. We were just passing a side street when a boy on a bicycle came out. Fred swung the wheel around to avoid hitting him. We missed the boy on the bicycle but hit another car that was trying to pass us.

HINT BANK

- shock〔ʃɑk〕*n.* （精神上的）打擊；（心的）震盪
- ***in the wrong*** 不對；錯誤　　***side street*** 巷道

不，是弗瑞德開車。當一個騎腳踏車的男孩出現時，我們正要過一個巷道。弗瑞德掉轉方向盤避免撞到他。我們閃過了騎腳踏車的男孩，可是撞到另外一輛想超我們車的車子。

中國人： Then it wasn't Fred's fault at all, was it?

那麼，一點都不是弗瑞德的錯了，不是嗎？

外國人： *No, I don't suppose it was.* But the man in the other car was awfully angry.

是的，我想一點也不是。不過，另一輛車裏的男人非常生氣。

中國人： But he's as much to blame because he tried to pass you. Was he hurt?

不過，他同樣應負責任，因爲他想超車。他受傷了嗎？

外國人： No, I was the only one that was hurt.

不，我是唯一受傷的人。

中國人： *It's a shame.* Does your arm hurt very much?

眞是遺憾，妳的手臂很痛嗎？

外國人： Not any more. 不再痛了。

中國人： Did you break it? 妳的手臂斷了嗎？

外國人： No. The doctor says the bone isn't broken. I think it should be all right in a few days.

沒有，醫生說骨頭沒斷。我想兩三天後應該會好。

HINT BANK─────────────

・ *as much* 同樣地　　*in a few days* 近日中；兩三天之後

＊ "Does your arm hurt～?" 句中的 "hurt" 是指「痛」的意思。

中國人： You were lucky, weren't you? 妳很幸運，不是嗎？

外國人： I should say so. I was wearing a heavy coat. I think that saved me from having a broken arm.

　　　　我應該這麼說。我穿著一件很厚重的大衣。我想這救了我，使我免於斷一隻手臂。

中國人： Well, take care of yourself. I'll drop in again later this afternoon.

　　　　嗯，請保重自己。今天下午稍後，我會再來看你。

外國人： Thanks, Tina. *And say hello to the others for me.*

　　　　謝謝你，婷娜，替我跟其他人問候。

中國人： Yes, I will. Oh, I almost forgot to tell you. Charles left Taipei this morning for a trip to Kenting, and he asked me to give you his best.

　　　　是的，我會的。喔，我幾乎忘了告訴你。查理今天早上離開台北到墾丁渡假，他要我代他向你問候。

外國人： Thanks. But what made him think of making a trip to Kenting now? I know he's broke.

　　　　謝謝，不過，他怎麼會想現在到墾丁旅行呢？我知道他破產了。

中國人： I don't know the reason. Probably nobody knows except Charles himself. Anyway he says he'll be back early next month. 我不知道原因。也許除了查理之外，沒有人知道。無論如何，他說下個月初，他會回來。

HINT BANK

- *say hello* 問候

* 向病人或受傷的人，說：「請保重。」是用 "Take care of yourself."

* "give you his best" 在 "best" 的後面省略了 "wishes" 或 "regards"。

外國人：I'll be looking forward to his return.　He owes me some money.　我盼望他回來。他欠我一些錢。

中國人：Well, I think I'd better be leaving now.　Goodbye, Caroline.　嗯，我想我最好是現在就離開。卡洛琳，再見。

外國人：Goodbye, Tina.　Thanks again for coming to see me.　再見，婷娜，再次謝謝你來看我。

HINT BANK————————————————

· *be looking forward to* 期待

＊ 表示「再次的感謝」用 "Thanks again～." 。

▲Second Week, Sixth Day▲

How to Explain Means, Measures and Ways

第二週，第六天　如何說明手段與方法

) BASIC DIALOGUES (

1. A : *How are you going to* Hawaii？ 你打算怎麼去夏威夷？

   B : I wanted to go by sea, but my wife insisted on going by air, so we decided to take the United Airlines.
      我想乘船去，不過我太太堅持搭飛機去，所以我們決定搭聯航。

2. A : Which is the shortest way to the ball park?
      到棒球場哪條路最近？

   B : Take N Avenue. 走N大道。

3. A : How did you make your travel arrangements?
      你是怎麼準備好去旅行的？

   B : I made my travel arrangements through my travel agent. 我是透過旅遊代理商來做好旅行籌劃的。

4. A : *What do you do with* this stick?
      你用這根棍子來做什麼？

B : I use it to open the upper window.
我用它來打開比較高一點的窗戶。

5. A : Could you send this parcel by special delivery?
你可否用限時專送寄這個包裹？

B : Certainly, sir. 當然，先生。

6. A : Please write down your name here with a pen.
請用鋼筆在這裏寫下你的名字。

B : I don't have a pen with me. May I use a pencil?
我沒有帶鋼筆。我可以用鉛筆嗎？

A : I'm afraid a pencil won't do. Please wait a moment.
I'll go and find a pen.
恐怕鉛筆不行。請等一下，我去找鋼筆來。

B : Thank you. 謝謝你。

7. A : *How did you* climb the cliff? 你怎麼爬上那座懸崖的？

B : I climbed it with a rope. 我用繩子爬上去的。

HINT BANK────────────────

- *by sea* 乘船；由海路　　*ball park* 棒球場
- *travel agent* 旅遊代理商；旅行社職員
- *special delivery* 限時專送 (= 〔英〕*express delivery*)
- cliff 〔klɪf〕*n.* (尤指海邊的)懸崖；絕壁 (= *precipice*)

* 問別人「打算用什麼方法到某地方？」的句型是 "How are you going to～?"。
  表示「手段、方法」的介系詞是用 " by "，如：" by air " (搭飛機)，" by
  rail " (搭船)。
* " avenue " 是大街道，在美國的城市中，" Avenue " 和 " Street " 常為縱橫相
  交。例如：New York 市中的 " Avenue " 是南北向，" Street " 是東西向。
* "What do you do with～?" 是詢問「用～來做什麼？」的意思。

8. A : I'll be glad to buy it if I can pay you on the installment plan.

我樂意買下它，如果我能用分期付款辦法付你錢的話。

B : We usually don't sell on the installment plan, but in
your case, we will make an exception.

通常我們是不用分期付款辦法賣的，不過，你的情形我們
可以例外。

9. A : I don't have that much cash. Will you accept a check？

我沒有那麼多現款，請你接受支票好嗎？

B : Certainly, sir. 當然，先生。

HINT BANK————————

- *installment plan* 分期付款辦法（＝〔英〕*hire-purchase system*）
- *make an exception* 給予特別優待

⊁ APPLIED CONVERSATION ⊁ 和將前往高雄的朋友交談

Talking to a Friend Who Is Going to Kaohsiung

外國人：Hello, Mary. I hear you're going to the south in a few days. 嗨，瑪莉。我聽說這幾天你要到南部。

中國人：Yes, Arthur. I have to make a business trip to Kaohsiung. I'm leaving on Thursday. 是的，亞瑟。我必須到高雄作一趟商業旅行。將在星期四離開。

外國人：Are you taking a plane? 你要搭飛機去嗎？

中國人：I wanted to go by plane, but I couldn't get a ticket. I suppose I'll have to go by train. 我要搭飛機去，但是，買不到機票。我大概必須搭火車去。

外國人：When will you be back? 你什麼時候回來？

中國人：I think I'll spend Sunday in Kaohsiung and fly back on Monday. 我想我會在高雄渡週日，星期一（搭飛機）飛回來。

外國人：Well, if you're not going to be here over the weekend, it **may be a good chance for me** to take that trip to Kenting National Park.

HINT BANK───────────────

- **in a few days** 二、三天

嗯，如果這個週末你不在這裏，那對我來說，可能是到墾丁
國家公園旅行的好機會。

中國人：Yes. **Why don't you go**? 好啊。你為什麼不去？

外國人：Do you think I should take my car?
你認為我應該自己開車嗎？

中國人：Well, I would advise you against it. It's much faster
if you take the train. The superhighway is so crowded that it will take you twice the time by car.
嗯，我反對。你如果搭火車會比較快。高速公路太擁擠，
搭車會花你兩倍的時間。

外國人：I guess you're right. But what if I want to go to a
few different places in the Kenting National Park area?
我想你說的沒錯。但是如果我想去墾丁國家公園的好幾個
不同的地方，怎麼辦？

中國人：There are plenty of taxis there. 那裡有很多計程車。

外國人：But I understand they're quite expensive — at least
more expensive than the taxis here in Taipei.
但是據我所知，計程車很貴——至少比台北這裡的計程車貴。

中國人：Then take a bus. They have excellent bus service all
over the Kenting National Park.
那麼搭巴士吧！墾丁國家公園到處都有很好的巴士服務。

HINT BANK────────────────

＊ "Why don't you go？" 這是句「鼓勵、勸誘」的話。

＊ "advise against～" 是表示「反對～」的意思。

＊ "I understand～." 在這裏是指「我聽說～。」的意思。

外國人：Where do you think is the best place to stay?
你認為哪裏是最好的投宿地點？

中國人：Well, if you want the best, you can stay at the
Caesar Park Hotel.
呃，如果你要最好的，你可以選擇凱撒大飯店。

外國人：Is there some place that's fairly reasonable and near
the beach? 有沒有哪裡價錢不貴又靠近海灘的？

中國人：Why don't you stay at Kenting Youth Activity Center?
那你何不住在墾丁青年活動中心？

外國人：Is it very expensive? 很貴嗎？

中國人：No, it's quite reasonable, and you'll be staying right
on the beach.
不，價錢相當合理，而且你住的地方就是在海灘上。

外國人：Good. I'll stay there. 好極了，我就去住那裡。

HINT BANK────────────────

• reasonable〔'riznəbl̩〕 *adj.*（價格等）不貴的；合理的

應答重點的強調

3rd Week   Hints on How to Ask and How to Request

Third Week, First Day

Basic Ways of Asking

第三週・第一天　基本的詢問方式

) BASIC DIALOGUES (

1. A : May I ask your name? 請問尊姓大名？

   B : My name is Brown...Peter Brown. 我叫布朗…彼得・布朗。

2. A : *Have you got the right time*? 你知道現在正確的時間嗎？

   B : It's just four o'clock. 正好四點。

3. A : Do you think it'll clear up tomorrow?
      你想明天會放晴嗎？

   B : Yes, I do. I think it will stop raining this evening.
      是的，我想會的。我想今天晚上雨就會停了。

4. A : I wonder if this bus will take us to Tamsui.
      不知道這輛巴士會不會載我們到淡水。

   B : I'm sure it will. 我確信它會的。

5. A : I'd like to know if I'm taking the right road to
      Hsimenting. 我想知道，我走的這條路是不是到西門町。

B : I'm afraid you've come the wrong way. You should
   have taken a left at the railroad crossing.
   恐怕你走錯路了。你應該在鐵路平交道的地方左轉。

6. A : Please tell me which is the shortest way to Shihlin.
   請告訴我到士林哪條路最近。

   B : Take this road until you come to the first traffic
   signal. Turn left, and in about 20 minutes you'll be
   in Shihlin. 往這條路直走，到了第一個交通信號燈，然後
   左轉，大約二十分鐘內，你就會到士林。

7. A : Do you know if this train will arrive in Taipei before
   noon? 你認為這班車在中午前會抵達台北嗎？

   B : I believe it won't. 我認為不會。

8. A : I've heard your sister is going to the United States
   to study there. Is that true?
   我聽說你妹妹將到美國唸書，眞的嗎？

   B : Yes, it's true. She's planning to stay there for about
   a year. 是的，是眞的。她計劃在那裏待大約一年。

HINT BANK————————————————

- *clear up* （天氣）放晴   crossing〔'krɔsɪŋ〕*n.* 平交道；十字路口
- *traffic signal* 交通信號（燈）   *arrive in* 到達（大地方）

* 請問別人尊姓大名時，較禮貌的詢問方式是"May I ask your name？"如果用
"Who are you？"或"What is your name？"聽起來較爲直接而且不客氣。

* "stop"有二種用法：① "stop ＋ V-ing"表示「停止 V-ing 的動作」。
② "stop ＋ to ＋ V"表示「停下來做 V 的動作」。

◀APPLIED CONVERSATION▶ 幫生病的朋友辦事

Doing Errands for a Sick Friend

外國人：Hello, Lily. 嗨，莉莉。

中國人：Oh, hello, Mary.

哦，嗨，瑪莉。

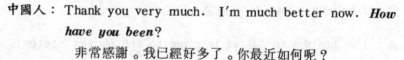

外國人：I heard you were sick, so
I've dropped in to see how
you are.

我聽說你病了，所以順道來

看看你怎麼樣了。

中國人：Thank you very much. I'm much better now. *How have you been*?

非常感謝。我已經好多了。你最近如何呢？

外國人：I've had a cold, but I'm all right now. Do you still have a fever?

我得了感冒，但是現在已經好了。你還在發燒嗎？

中國人：No, not any more. The doctor says I'll be able to go out in a few days.

不，沒有了。醫生說我這幾天就能出門了。

外國人：That's wonderful! Would you like me to do anything for you? 那太好了！你要我替你做什麼事嗎？

HINT BANK

· *go out* 外出

* " not any more " 是 " I do not have a fever any more." 的省略。

中國人： No, I can't think of anything...Oh, yes, will you *do me one small favor*?

不，我想不起有什麼…噢，對了，你能幫我一個小忙嗎？

外國人： Why, of course. What is it? 噢，當然可以。幫什麼忙？

中國人： I left a pair of shoes at the repair shop just around the corner. Could you pick them up for me?

我有雙鞋子放在街角處的修理店裡，你能把它們帶來給我嗎？

外國人： Of course. What kind of shoes are they?

當然，那是雙怎樣的鞋子？

中國人： Oh, just ordinary walking shoes...brown and low heels.

哦，只是普通的散步鞋…咖啡色和低跟的。

外國人： All right. Did you say the repair shop is just around the corner? 好的。你說那修理店就在街角嗎？

中國人： Yes. It's next door to the tea shop we went to together the other day.

是的。就在幾天前我們一起去過的茶館的隔壁。

外國人： I see. *Is there anything else I can do*?

我知道了。還有什麼要幫忙的嗎？

中國人： No, thanks. 沒有，謝了。

HINT BANK

· *pick up* 拾起；順便帶…

* " do one a favor " 是指「幫某人的忙」。

* " low heels " 是指「低跟的鞋子」，要注意要用 " heels " 複數形來表示。

* 為了慎重起見，再問一遍對方曾說過的話，所用的句型是 " Did you say～? "

外國人： I'll get the shoes and bring them back. ***Will that be all right***?

　　　　我會去拿鞋子，然後把它們帶回來。這樣可以嗎？

中國人： Yes, and thanks so much. 是的，非常謝謝。

外國人： Don't mention it. I'll be back in a few minutes.

　　　　別客氣。我會在幾分鐘內回來。

中國人： Oh, wait a minute. Will you mail this letter for me? I wrote it yesterday, but I forgot to have it mailed.

　　　　哦，等一下，可以幫我寄這封信嗎？我昨天寫的，但是，忘了寄。

外國人： All right. 好的。

中國人： Do you think it will be delivered by tomorrow evening?

　　　　你認爲信在明天晚上之前會送到嗎？

外國人： I'm not sure. Would you like it to be sent special delivery? 我不確定。你要寄限時專送嗎？

中國人： Yes. 是的。

外國人： All right. I'll be back soon. 好。我很快就回來。

HINT BANK

・ ***wait a minute*** 稍等；等一下　　***special delivery*** 限時專送

＊ "Will that be all right？" 是 "Is that all right？" 的未來式，是客氣地詢問「對方的意圖、打算」。

Grammar and Usage

1. 基本疑問句型

　　最簡單的疑問句型是把"You are～."換成"Are you～?"但是，此型只限於"be"動詞和"have"動詞。

2. 以助動詞為句首的句型

　　一般動詞在句首加"Do"或"Does"，就是疑問句。如：

- He lives in Taipei.（他住在台北。）
　→*Does* he live in Taipei?（他住在台北嗎？）

同樣地，將"can","may","will","shall"等助動詞放在句首，也可形成疑問句。如：

- *Can* you play the piano?（你會彈琴嗎？）
- *Will* he come tomorrow?（他明天會來嗎？）

3. 以疑問詞為句首的句型

　　上面所敘述的句型，全以"Yes."或"No."回答。但是，如果以疑問詞，如："who","which","what","when"等為疑問句，則不能用"Yes.","No."回答。

- *Who* is that gentleman?（那位是誰？）

4. 含有命令句的句型

　　有些句子形式上是命令句，但是表達的內容和疑問句相同，是要求對方回答。這類句型，大部分用在"(Please) tell me～."上。如：

- *Tell me* which is the shortest way to Hsimenting.
　（請告訴我到西門町最快的路。）

Third Week, Second Day

Polite Ways of Asking

第三週，第二天　客氣的詢問方式

BASIC DIALOGUES

1. A : Would you kindly tell me how to get to your office?
　　　請你告訴我怎麼到你的辦公室好嗎？

B : Of course. Take the bus that goes to Jingmei and
get off at National Taiwan University. My office
is just in front of the bus stop, so *you can't miss it*.
　　　當然可以。搭往景美的公車，在台灣大學下車。我的辦公
室就在公車站前面，所以你不會找不到的。

2. A : If you will excuse me, I'd like to ask if this train will
stop at Taichung?
　　　對不起打擾了，我想請問你這班火車在台中停不停？

B : Yes, it will. I think it'll arrive at Taichung around
5 : 30.
　　　是的，有停。我想這班火車大約五點三十分會到台中。

3. A： *I beg your pardon*, may I ask you to close the window？
　　　抱歉，可以請你關上窗戶嗎？

　　B： Certainly, yes. 是的，當然可以。

4. A： Excuse me, sir, could you tell me where I can get a
　　　ticket for Tainan？
　　　先生，對不起，請你告訴我什麼地方可以買到台南的車票？

　　B： Certainly. You can get your ticket at Window No.12
　　　or 13. 當然可以。你可以在12或13號窗口買到車票。

5. A： May I ask you a question, please？我可以請教個問題嗎？

　　B： Of course. What is it？可以。是什麼問題呢？

　　A： I'd like to know if any of Dr. Lin Yutang's novels are
　　　published in English.
　　　我想知道是否有林語堂博士英文版的小說。

　　B： I remember I read one of his novels in English. I
　　　think the title was "Peking Story."
　　　我記得我讀過他英文版的一本小說。我想書名是「京華煙
　　　雲」。

HINT BANK ─────────────────────

＊ "You can't miss it." 是表示「你不會找不到的。」，"miss" 在此是指「錯
過；看漏」的意思。

＊ "Certainly, yes." 句中的 "Certainly" 是針對 "May I ask～？" 的回答，而
"yes" 是表示「可以關窗」。全句所表達的是「當然可以。」更輕鬆的講法是
只用 "Sure."

＊ "any of～" 是指「任何其中之一」的意思。

◀ APPLIED CONVERSATION ▶ 在旅館的大廳

In a Hotel Lobby

外國人： **May I introduce myself?**

My name is George Smith.

請容我自我介紹。

我的名字叫喬治‧史密斯。

中國人： It's a pleasure to meet you, Mr. Smith. My name is Thomas.

很高興見到你，史密斯先生。

我的名字叫湯瑪斯。

外國人： Thomas？ I'm very happy to meet you.

湯瑪斯？我很高興見到你。

中國人： Is this your first trip to Taiwan, Mr. Smith？

史密斯先生，這是你第一次來台灣旅行嗎？

外國人： Yes, it is. **Everything is new to me.** Incidentally, if it isn't too much trouble, could you show me the way to Hsimenting？

是的。對我來說每件事情都是新奇的。如果不麻煩的話，順便請你教我到西門町的路好嗎？

中國人： Why, of course. Would you like me to draw a map for you？ 當然可以。你要我為你畫一張地圖給你嗎？

HINT BANK ────────────────

· incidentally 〔͵ɪnsə'dɛntl̩ɪ 〕 *adv.* 讓我順便一提

外國人：Yes, that would be a great help. I could just show it to the taxi driver.

好的，那將有很大的幫助。我正好可以拿地圖給計程車司機看。

中國人：Exactly where is it you wish to go in the Hsimenting district? 你想到西門町的哪一個確定地方？

外國人：I understand there is a street called Movie Street. Do you know where it is?

我知道有條街叫電影街。你知道在哪裏嗎？

中國人：Oh, yes. It's a very well-known place. I don't think you'll need a map. Just tell the driver to take you to Movie Street.

噢，知道。那是很有名的地方。我想你不需要地圖了。只要告訴司機帶你到電影街就好了。

外國人：I see. Will that get me there?

我知道了。那樣我就可以到那裏了嗎？

中國人：Yes, any taxi driver will know.

是的，任何一個計程車司機都知道。

外國人：Fine. Oh, and there's one other thing I'd like to ask you, if I may.

很好。哦，如果可以的話，我還有一件事想請問你。

中國人：Of course. 當然可以。

HINT BANK

* "any taxi driver will know" 句中用 "will" 並不是表示未來，而是指「應該（知道）」。

外國人： I'm asking an American couple to have dinner with me this evening. Could you suggest a good restaurant？

我今晚邀了一對美國夫婦共餐。請你介紹一家好的餐館好嗎？

中國人： Well, there are so many good places to eat. Would you want to take them to a Japanese style restaurant, Chinese style, French, Indian...？

噢，有很多好的地方可以用餐。你想帶他們去日本式餐館，或是中國式、法國式、印度式餐館呢？

外國人： Well, since I don't speak Chinese, perhaps I'd better take them to a western style restaurant.

噢，因爲我不會說中國話，或許帶他們去西餐廳比較好。

中國人： *Do you care for French food*？ There's an excellent French restaurant not far from this hotel.

你喜歡吃法國菜嗎？這家旅館不遠的地方有一家很好的法國餐館。

外國人： Is it within walking distance？ 走路就可以到嗎？

中國人： Yes, it's about a 10-minute walk. Shall I draw you a map？ 是的，大約要走10分鐘的路。我畫一張地圖給你好嗎？

外國人： Yes, I would appreciate that. 好的，我很感激。

中國人： Here you are. 在這裏。

外國人： Thank you so much. You've been very helpful.

非常謝謝。你幫我太多忙了。

HINT BANK

• *care for* ～〔用於否定、疑問句〕想（要）；喜歡

* "good places to eat" 是 "good places where you can eat" 的意思。

Grammar and Usage

　　疑問句型，依其用法不同，可作爲客氣有禮貌的表達，或作爲不客氣的問法。爲了避免誤用，以下說明幾種有禮貌的疑問句。

1. *Would you kindly tell me ～*?

　　" Would you ～?" 的 " would " 本來是假設法的一種。表示「如果可以的話～」的意思。所以是屬於很有禮貌的表達方式。

2. *If you will excuse me ～*?

　　按照字面是指「假如你能原諒我的話」，常用在「拜託別人」或「發問」。但是，也可以更簡單地以 " Excuse me, but ～?" 來表達。

- *Excuse me, but* could you tell me where I can find the elevators?（對不起，不過你能不能告訴我電梯在哪裏?）

和此意思相同的用法有 " I beg your pardon, ～."

3. *May I ask ～*?"

　　用 " Who are you?" 問「你是誰?」是非常不禮貌的。因爲這含有盤問的口氣。較有禮貌的說法是用 " May I ask ～?" 的句型。如：

- *May I ask* your name?（請問尊姓大名?）

4. 其他句型

　　用 " can "，" may "，" will " 等助動詞的過去式，來表示禮貌的用法。例如用 " *Could* you direct me to Taipei Station?"（你能不能告訴我如何到台北火車站?）的問法，比用 " Can you direct me to Taipei Station?" 聽起來較有禮貌。

◣Third Week, Third Day◢

How to Ask Permission

第三週，第三天　如何要求許可

▶ BASIC DIALOGUES ◀

1. A : May I borrow this book？我可以借這本書嗎？

   B : Yes, of course. 當然可以 。

2. A : Can I take this, please？ 我可以拿這個東西嗎？

   B : Certainly. 當然可以 。

3. A : *Is it all right for me* to play some cassette tapes on your stereo？ 我可以在你的立體音響放卡式錄音帶嗎 ？

   B : Sure！當然！

4. A : Would it be all right if I took your picture？
        如果我替你照像可以嗎？

   B : Why, of course. 哦，當然可以 。

5. A : I'd like to have a few words with him if I may.
        如果可以，我想跟他說幾句話 。

B : I'm afraid he's too busy now.
　　恐怕他現在很忙。

6. A : Do you mind if I use this telephone?
　　　你介意我用這隻電話嗎？

B : Not at all. Please go ahead. 一點也不，請用。

7. A : Would you mind if I went out for a walk?
　　　你介意我出去散步嗎？

B : No. Of course not. I wonder if I could go with you.
　　　不，當然不會。我不知是否可以跟你一起去。

A : Sure. 當然。

8. A : *I wonder if you'd mind* my opening the window.
　　　不知你是否介意我打開窗戶。

B : Please don't. I have a cold. 請不要，我感冒了。

9. A : Could you allow us to take a rest?
　　　請你允許我們休息一下好嗎？

B : OK. Let's all take a ten-minute break.
　　　好的。讓我們都休息十分鐘。

HINT BANK ─────────────────

- cassette〔kæ'sɛt〕*n.* (裝錄音帶等的)卡式盒
- stereo〔'stɛrɪo, 'stɪrɪo〕*n.* 立體音響設備(如電唱機等)

＊ 表示「請求別人許可」的簡單句型有："May I～?"和"Can I～?"

＊ "Would it be all right if I took your picture?" 在 if 子句中用過去式，
　是表示禮貌的用法。

＊ 用"Do you mind if～?"問，回答"Not at all." 是表示「當然可以。」

＊ "I wonder if I could～?"是委婉請求許可的說法。

10. A： Will you let me use your typewriter？

你可以讓我用你的打字機嗎？

B： Yes, please do. 好的，請用。

11. A： May I have permission to leave a little early this afternoon？ 今天中午我可以提早走嗎？

B： All right, but perhaps you'd better ask Mr. Cooper, too. 好的，但是你最好也去問一下庫柏先生。

HINT BANK

* permission〔pə'mɪʃən〕 *n.* 許可；允許

* 「請求別人許可」時，用 " May I have permission to～？" 是屬於較正式的用法。

⋈ APPLIED CONVERSATION ⋈ 用電話邀約

Making an Appointment by Telephone

中國人：Hello. Is this the Brown
　　　　residence?
　　　　喂。這是布朗公館嗎？

外國人：Yes, this is Mrs. Brown
　　　　speaking.
　　　　是的，我是布朗太太。

中國人：Oh, hello, Helen. This is
　　　　Kay. 哦，哈囉，海倫。我是
　　　　凱伊。

外國人：Hello, Kay. How are you? 哈囉，凱伊。你好嗎？

中國人：Quite well, thank you. I called to ask whether it
　　　　would be all right for me to visit you tomorrow.
　　　　很好，謝謝你。我打電話來問明天拜訪你是否適合。

外國人：Why, certainly. What time will you be coming?
　　　　當然可以。你什麼時候會來？

中國人：***Will three o'clock be convenient for you***?
　　　　三點鐘時你方便嗎？

外國人：Yes, I'll be in all afternoon. 方便，我整個下午都在。

HINT BANK ─────────────────

- residence〔'rɛzədəns〕*n.* 住宅；住處

* 「我是～。」在電話用語中是 "This is ～ speaking." 也可以省略，只用
　"Speaking."

中國人： I wonder if you'd mind if I brought my kid sister
along. You see, she's staying with us for a few days.
不知道你介不介意，我帶我的小妹一塊兒去。你知道，她
這幾天要跟我們在一塊兒。

外國人： Why, of course not. I'd love to meet her.
當然不介意。我喜歡見到她。

中國人： And *I'd like to ask another favor of you*, if I may.
如果可以，我想還要請你幫個忙。

外國人： Yes, what is it? 好的，是什麼呢？

中國人： You see, my sister is quite interested in cooking and
I wondered if you'd mind giving her some of your re-
cipes. 你知道，我的妹妹對烹飪很有興趣，我想你是否願
意教她一些烹飪方法。

外國人： Why, not at all. Is she interested in anything particular? 當然可以。她對什麼事特別感興趣嗎？

中國人： Well, she's interested in baking bread and cakes just
at the moment. You see, she has a new oven.
噢，現在她對烤麵包和蛋糕有興趣。你知道，她有一台新
的烤箱。

外國人： If you have the time, *why don't you stay for dinner*?
I could show her how to bake a cake.
如果你有時間，為什麼不留下來吃晚餐呢？我可以教她如
何烤蛋糕。

HINT BANK────────────────

• recipe〔'rɛsəpɪ,-,pi〕*n.* 烹飪法   particular〔pə'tɪkjələ,pə-〕*adj.* 特別的

中國人：But wouldn't that be putting you to too much trouble?
但是那不會給你太多的麻煩嗎？

外國人：Not at all. You know how I like to cook. I think it will be fun.
一點也不會。你知道我是多麼喜歡烹飪。我認為會很有趣的。

中國人：It's awfully kind of you to say so. Are you sure it won't be too much trouble?
你這麼說真好。你確定不會給你太多的麻煩嗎？

外國人：*Now don't you worry about it*, Kay. Just bring your sister and be here at three o'clock.
現在你不要擔心這個，凱伊。只要三點鐘時帶着你的妹妹來這裡就好了。

中國人：Thank you so much, Helen. We'll be there.
太謝謝你了，海倫。我們會去的。

外國人：Fine. Goodbye, Kay. 很好。再見，凱伊。

中國人：Goodbye, Helen. 再見，海倫。

HINT BANK ───────────────

* "Why don't you stay for dinner?" 用 "why" 並不是表示疑問，而是含有勸誘的意味。

* "Just bring～." 句中的 "just" 是為緩和命令語氣而添加的。在會話中，常用到 "just" 這個字。

◤ Third Week, Fourth Day ◢

How to Request or Entrust

第三週，第四天　如何請求或委託

◖ BASIC DIALOGUES ◗

1. A : Will you please open the window? 麻煩你開窗好嗎？

　　B : All right. 好的。

2. A : Won't you please stop smoking in here?
　　　　請你不要在這裏抽烟好嗎？

　　B : Yes, sir. 是的，先生。

3. A : Would you please wake me up at six tomorrow morning?
　　　　請你明天早上六點叫醒我好嗎？

　　B : Yes, I will. 好的，我會的。

4. A : Would you help me with my French lesson, please?
　　　　請你幫我做法文功課好嗎？

　　B : I'm afraid I can't now. Can't you possibly do it by
　　　　yourself today? 恐怕我現在不能。你今天不可能自己做嗎？

　　A : Of course I can. 當然我能。

5. A : Could you give me a call early next week?
   　　可否請你下星期一、二（初）給我一通電話？

   B : Surely.　I'll call you Monday morning.
   　　當然，下星期一早上我會打電話給你。

6. A : *Would you mind* closing the door?
   　　請你把那扇門關起來好嗎？

   B : Not at all. 好的。

7. A : I'd like to ask you to write a letter for me, if you
   　　don't mind. 我想請你幫我寫封信，如果你不介意的話。

   B : It's a pleasure. 這是我的榮幸。

8. A : Would you drop this letter in a mail box somewhere
   　　along the way?
   　　請你幫我把這封信投進沿途某處的郵筒裏好嗎？

   B : Of course. 當然。

9. A : I'd be grateful if you would lend me this book.
   　　如果你願意借這本書給我的話，我會很感激的。

   B : I'd be glad to. 我很樂意。

HINT BANK ————————————————————

- *give ~ a call* 打電話給~

* 「拜託或請求別人」的句型有：" Will you please ~? ", " Won't you please
  ~ ? "和" Would you please ~ ? "。其中以用" Would you please ~ ? "的
  句型最爲有禮貌。

* " Would you mind ~ ? "是表示「請你~好嗎？」的意思。如果回答「好的。」
  是用" Not at all. "或" Certainly not. "。

◀ APPLIED CONVERSATION ▶ 請求朋友寫介紹信
Asking a Friend to Write an Introduction

外國人： Good morning, David. *I dropped in to ask you a favor.* 早安，大衛，我來請你幫個忙。

中國人： Of course. What can I do for you? 當然，有什麼我可以效勞的？

外國人： Well, I want to go to the Pacific Trading Company with a proposal I think they'll be interested in. Do you know anyone over there?
　　　　嗯，我想帶一個案子到太平洋貿易公司，我想他們會感興趣的。你認識那裏的任何人嗎？

中國人： I know several people. I know Mr. Lee quite well. He's the head of the sales department.
　　　　我認識幾個人。我跟李先生相當熟，他是銷售部門的主管。

外國人： He would be just the person. Could you give me a letter of introduction?
　　　　他就是我要找的人，可否請你給我一封介紹信？

中國人： Why, certainly. *I'd be most happy to.*
　　　　哦，當然，我樂意之至。

HINT BANK —————————

　　• *ask one a favor* 向某人拜託事情　　proposal〔prə'pozl〕*n.* 提案；計劃

外國人： I'd be grateful if you could mention in the letter the fact that your company and mine are close business associates. 如果你能在信裏面提及，我們兩家公司是很親密的生意夥伴，我會非常感激。

中國人： Of course. Can you think of anything else I should put in the letter? 當然。你可否想想，其他事情我應該寫到信裏面去的？

外國人： Well, you might mention that we're very good personal friends. 嗯，你可以提我們私底下是非常好的朋友。

中國人： Yes, of course. All right, here you are. 是的，當然。好的，這就是。

外國人： I can't tell you how much I appreciate this. 我無法告訴你，我是多麼欣賞這封信。

中國人： Don't mention it. *It's the least I can do for a friend.* By the way, you can do me a favor in return. 不客氣，這是我為朋友起碼可以做到的。順便一提，你能幫我個忙作為回報嗎？

外國人： Sure, anything. What is it? 當然，任何事情。是什麼忙？

中國人： You're coming to the small dinner party I'm giving next Saturday night, aren't you? 你要參加下星期六晚上我辦的一個小型宴會，不是嗎？

HINT BANK──────────────

- associate 〔əˈsoʃɪɪt〕 *n.* 夥伴 　　　*personal friend* 私交不錯的朋友
- *in return* 作為回報；以為回答 　　　*dinner party* 宴會；晚宴

外國人： Yes, of course. 是的，當然。

中國人： Well, I've also asked Joan Richards to come. I wonder
if I could ask you to pick her up and bring her to my
house...and also take her home after the party.

嗯，我也請瓊安‧理查斯來。不知道我是否可以請你去接
她，並且帶她來我家…而且宴會完也帶她回家。

外國人： Do you mean the very pretty chick we met at the
Country Club dance？

你是指我們在鄉村俱樂部舞會上，遇見的那位美麗的少女？

中國人： Yes, the one who works as an art designer.

是的，那位當藝術設計家的女孩。

外國人： By all means！當然可以！

中國人： Well, I'm glad you see it that way.

嗯，我很高興你這麼認為。

外國人： But I don't know her telephone number. Could you
give it to me？

不過我不知道她的電話號碼，可否請你給我她的電話號碼？

中國人： Yes, of course. 525-6211. 是的，當然，五二五六二一一。

外國人： I got it. Well, thanks for everything, David.

我知道了，嗯，一切都謝謝你，大衞。

HINT BANK ──────────────

・ chick〔 tʃɪk 〕*n.* 少女

＊ "Do you mean～?"（你是說～?），也可以直接用 "You mean～?"

＊ "by all means" 是指「一定；當然；無論如何一定」，用在加強回答的語氣。

＊ "I got it." 是「我知道了。」也可以用 "understood" 來代替 "got"。

Grammar and Usage

1. *Will you*（*please*）～？

"Will you（please）～？"是最常用的請託句型。但是，要注意的是，"Will you～？"有時只是單純表示未來式。如：

- *Will* you be free tomorrow night？
  （明晚你有空嗎？）→未來式

- *Will* you open the window？（打開窗戶好嗎？）→請託句型

比"Will you～？"更有禮貌的用法是"Won't you（please）～？"而最有禮貌的用法是"Would you（please）～？"

2. 其他使用 *would* 的句型

"would"常用在客氣的表達上，其中最具代表性的句型是"Would you mind～ing？"和"I wish you would～."

- *Would you mind* shutting the window？（你介意關上窗戶嗎？）

另外，"I wish you would～."（希望你能～。）也是很有禮貌的委託、請求的句型。和此用法類似的有"I'd like to ask you～."（我想要拜託你～。）

3. 使用 *if* 來表達請託的句型

這種句型有"I'd be grateful *if* you would（could, might）～."和"I wonder *if* you would（could, might）～."前面句中的"I'd be grateful～."還可用"I'd appreciate it～."或"I'd be very happy～."來代換。這些都是禮貌的用法。

4. 對別人請託的回答

對上面各種請託的句型，回答時可用"All right."或"Of course.","I'd be glad to."或"It's a pleasure."等等。

◢ Third Week, Fifth Day ◣

How to Propose, Advise or Invite

第三週・第五天　如何建議、勸告或邀請

▶ BASIC DIALOGUES ◀

1. A : Let's go to the movies, okay? 我們去看電影，好嗎？

　　B : Yes, let's. 好的，咱們走。

2. A : Should we take the bus ? 我們搭公車好嗎？

　　B : No. Let's take a taxi. It's much faster.

　　　　不，我們搭計程車，計程車比較快。

3. A : *How about* having lunch together ? 一起吃午餐怎麼樣？

　　B : That's a good idea. 好主意。

4. A : *What do you think of* going to Hsimenting together ?

　　　　一起去西門町如何？

　　B : I'm afraid I can't go out. I'm expecting a call from

　　　　John this afternoon.

　　　　恐怕我不能外出，我正等著約翰今天下午的電話。

5. A： You'd better take your umbrella with you. 你最好帶傘。

　　B： Thank you, I will. 謝謝，我會的。

6. A： *Had you better* call up your mother and tell her you're going to be late?

　　　　 你最好打電話給你母親，告訴她你會遲到？

　　B： Yes. That's a good idea. 好的。好主意。

7. A： Why don't you ask for Mr. Thomas' help？

　　　　 你為什麼不請湯瑪斯幫忙？

　　B： Do you really think he would？

　　　　 你真的以為他會幫忙嗎？

8. A： We would be very happy if you could come to our house for dinner next Friday evening.

　　　　 如果你下星期五晚上能來我們家吃晚餐，我們將會很高興的。

　　B： Why, it's nice of you to ask. I'd be most happy to go.

　　　　 哦，謝謝你的好意，我會很高興去的。

HINT BANK ────────────────────────

* "Let's go to ~, okay？" 用 "okay" 比用 "shall we" 更口語化。
* 表示「提議」的常用句型有：" How about ~ ？" 和 " What do you think of ~ ？"

⫷ APPLIED CONVERSATION ⫸ 關於聖誕舞會的建議
Giving Advice for a Christmas Party

安 迪：Say, David, Mary and I are
planning to have some friends
in for a little Christmas party.
I want to ask your advice about
inviting certain people that
you know quite well.

喂，大衞，瑪莉和我正計劃邀請
幾位朋友在家開個小型的聖誕舞
會。對於要邀請你所熟悉的人，
我想聽聽你的意見。

中國人：Sure, Andy, I'd be glad to. But it's your party, why
don't you invite just the people you know well ?

當然，安迪，我很樂意。但是這是你們開的舞會，為什麼不
邀請你較熟悉的人呢？

瑪 莉：We are, but there are some we'd like to invite that
you know better than we do.

我們是這麼做，但是一些我們想要邀請的人,你比我們更熟。

中國人：All right, which are the ones you want to ask me about?

好的，哪些人是你們想要問我的？

安 迪：First of all, George and Kay.

首先，要邀請的是喬治和凱伊。

HINT BANK————————————————————

* " have some friends in "句中的 " in "是指「在家」的意思。

中國人： Oh, they're an awfully nice couple. They'd fit in any
place and I'm sure they'd love to come.

　　哦，他們是好得不得了的一對。他們到什麼地方，都和別人
　　合得來，我確定他們會喜歡來的。

安　迪： Good. 好。

瑪　莉： And there's Alice. What about her ?

　　還有愛麗絲。她怎麼樣？

中國人： Well, if you invite Alice, you should invite Frank, too.
I think they'll be tying the knot soon.

　　好，如果你邀請愛麗絲，你也應該邀請富蘭克。我想他們很
　　快就要結婚了。

瑪　莉： Well, we don't know Frank, but we'd be glad to have
him come.

　　好的，雖然我們不認識富蘭克，但是我們歡迎他來。

中國人： Do you have Bob on your list ?

　　鮑伯有沒有在你的名單上呢？

安　迪： Yes, he was the next name on our list. What do you
advise about him ?

　　有的，他是我們名單上的下一位。你對他有何意見？

中國人： By all means give him an invitation. *He's lots of fun
at parties.* 無論如何要邀請他，他在舞會上會很有趣的。

HINT BANK————————————————

・ knot〔nɑt〕 *n.* 婚姻結合

＊ “ fit in any place ”是指「適合任何地方」也就是指「到什麼地方，都和別人
　合得來」。

安　迪：Good. We'll send him an invitation.
　　　　好的。我們會給他一封邀請函。

瑪　莉：Now, what about Bill? 現在，比爾怎麼樣呢？

中國人：Well, Bill's no problem when he's sober, but if he has too many drinks he's liable to become a pest.
　　　　嗯，當比爾清醒的時候他沒有問題，但是如果他喝了太多酒，他就可能變成一個討厭的人。

安　迪：Well, do you think we'd better leave him out?
　　　　哦，你想我們是不是最好刪除他？

中國人：*It's up to you*, but I would.
　　　　由你決定，但是我會刪除他。

瑪　莉：Well, we'll take your advice. 好的，我們採取你的意見。

安　迪：I guess that completes the list. Are there any other names you can suggest?
　　　　我猜想名單已經完成了。有沒有其他的人你可以建議的？

中國人：I suppose you have Jack on the list.
　　　　我想名單上有傑克。

瑪　莉：Yes. We wouldn't forget Jack. *He's the life of the party*. 是的，我們不要忘了傑克，他是舞會裏的靈魂人物。

中國人：I guess that's all, then. 那麼，我想已經足夠了。

安　迪：Thanks a lot. 多謝了。

HINT BANK——————————

- sober〔'sobɚ〕*adj.* 未醉的；清醒的　　*be liable to* ~ 易於~
- pest〔pɛst〕*n.* 令人討厭的人或物

* "I guess that's all." 句中的 "I guess" 是美國人常用的口語，意思和 "I think" 一樣。

Grammar and Usage

表示提議、忠告、勸誘的說法，有許多共同點，現將這類句型略述如下：

1. *Let's ～.* 和 *Shall we ～*？

以 " Let's " 爲句首，在後面加 " shall we？" 是用來詢問對方的意向、打算。

・Let's go to the movies together, *shall we*？
（我們一起去看電影，好吧？）

只用 " Shall we ～？" 也可以表達和用 " Let's ～, shall we？" 相同的意思。另外，比較輕鬆的說法是用 " Let's ～, okay？"

對於 " Let's ～,（shall we？)" 或 " Shall we ～？" 的肯定回答通常用 " Yes, let's.",否定回答則用 " No, let's not."

2. *How about ～*？

這是「～如何？」的意思，常在勸誘對方時使用。在 " about " 後面接動名詞（V＋ing)或名詞。如果只接名詞也可用作詢問對方的意見。

・*How about* having a cup of coffee？（來杯咖啡如何？）
・*How about* tomorrow？（明天如何？）

3. 用 *had better* 表示忠告

" had better " 是「最好～」的意思。後面不加 " to"。表示否定時，用 " had better not＋動詞"。" You had better（not)～." 有點近似命令的語氣，所以，對長輩的忠告，不可用這句話。

▌Third Week, Sixth Day▙

How to Chime in with, or Echo Another's Words

第三週，第六天　如何表示贊同或附和

▌ BASIC DIALOGUES ▐

1. **A** : Taipei is one of the most interesting cities in the
world. 台北市是世界上最有趣的城市之一 。

   B : *Do you really think so*? 你眞的認為如此嗎？

2. **A** : I think we'd better begin our tour around Taipei at
the National Palace Museum.

   　　我想我們最好從國立故宮博物院開始我們的台北旅遊 。

   B : Why not the Chung Cheng Memorial Hall？It's closer.
為什麼不從中正紀念堂開始？它比較近 。

3. **A** : We should spend at least two days in Taipei.
　　我們至少應該花兩天的時間遊覽台北 。

   B : I agree. It's almost impossible to see Taipei in one
day. 我同意 。幾乎不可能一天之內遊覽完台北 。

   A : Maybe we should spend a week. Do we have the time？
也許我們應該花一個星期 。我們有時間嗎？

4. B：I think we ought to take the earliest train.

　　　我想我們應該搭最早班的火車。

　　A：Yeah. The earlier, the better.

　　　是的。愈早愈好。

5. B：He might enjoy his stay in Taiwan more fully if he could speak Chinese.

　　　如果他會說中文，他待在台灣可能更盡興。

　　A：***There's no doubt about it.***

　　　這是毫無疑問的。

6. B：It's my opinion that Chinese is one of the most difficult languages for foreigners to learn.

　　　依我的看法，中文對外國人來說，是最困難的語言之一。

　　A：***You can say that again!***

　　　也可以這麼說！（我有同感！）

7. B：English is the most important language in the world.

　　　英語是世界上最重要的語言。

　　A：At least it's the most popular. 至少它最普遍。

HINT BANK ————————————————————

· interesting〔ˊɪntrɪstɪŋ〕*adj.* 令人發生興趣的；有趣味的

· memorial〔məˊmorɪəl〕*adj.* 紀念的

· yeah〔jɛ；jæ〕*adv.* 〔美俗〕是的（= *yes*）

* "our tour around Taipei" 是指「遊覽台北」。

* "Do we have the time?" 也可以說成 "Can we spare the time?"

* 用 "He might ~ if he could" 的句型，是表示事實上並非如此。

⟫ APPLIED CONVERSATION ⟪ 商 談

A Business Discussion

中國人1 : Good morning, Mr. Baker.
I'm so glad you were able
to drop in this morning.
貝克爾先生，早安。我很高
興你今天早上能來看我。

貝克爾 : My pleasure, Mr. Wang.
Mr. Wang, this is my as-
sistant, John Carter. He's
the head of our Purchasing
Department. John, this is Mr. Wang.

這是我的榮幸，王先生。王先生，這位是我的助理，約翰·
卡特。他是我們採購部門的主任。約翰，這位是王先生。

卡　特 : *It's a pleasure to meet you*, Mr. Wang.
很榮幸認識你，王先生。

中國人1 : I'm happy to meet you, Mr. Carter. Now, if we
can wait for one moment...I'm expecting my sales
chief, Mr. Lee, to join us. Oh, here he is.
很高興認識你，卡特先生。如果我們能夠等一會兒…我在
等我的行銷主管李先生來加入我們。喔，他來了。

HINT BANK ────────────────

• purchase〔'pɝtʃəs, -ɪs〕*v.* 購買

中國人2 ： I'm sorry to have kept you waiting. How do you do, Mr. Baker. How are you today, Mr. Carter?
很抱歉讓你們久等了。幸會，貝克爾先生。你好嗎，卡特先生。

卡　　特 ： Fine, thank you. 我很好，謝謝你。

中國人1 ： Well, shall we get down to business?
那麼，我們開始談生意吧！

貝克爾 ： That's what we're here for, Mr. Wang.
那是我們來此的目的，王先生。

中國人1 ： I presume you've gone over the contract papers.
Are they satisfactory?
我想你已經看過合約書了，你滿意嗎？

貝克爾 ： There are one or two points I'd like to mention if I may. 如果可以的話，有一、兩點我想提出來。

中國人1 ： Certainly. 當然可以。

貝克爾 ： First, I believe the contract states that your initial delivery of 1,000 units will be made within two weeks of the signing of the contract. 首先，我想合約上說，第一批的一千件，將在合約簽訂後，兩星期內交貨。

中國人1 ： Yes, I believe that's correct.
是的，我想合約上是這麼說的。

HINT BANK ──────────────

• ***get down to*** (***one's work***) 靜下心（工作）；處理
• presume〔prɪˈzum〕v. 假定；推測　　***go over*** 重讀；複習
• state〔stet〕v. 說；陳述　　delivery〔dɪˈlɪvərɪ〕n. 交貨

貝克爾 ： ***I wonder if you couldn't*** give us the first 1,000 units within one week.

我想知道首批的一千件，是否能在一星期內交貨。

中國人1 ： That will make it quite a rush job. I'm afraid it will be a little difficult.

那將會很趕。恐怕有點困難。

中國人2 ： We would prefer to have two weeks ***if you can manage***.

如果可以設法的話，我們希望是兩個星期。

卡　特 ： You see, we have a buyer that wants 1,000 units immediately and we'd like to fill that order ***if it's at all possible***.

你知道，我們有位買主急著購買一千件，如果可能的話，我們想接受這批訂貨。

中國人1 ： Well, if it's that urgent, perhaps we can find some way of letting you have the first 1,000 units immediately.

哦，如果真的那麼緊急的話，也許我們可以想辦法很快地給你們首批一千件的貨。

貝克爾 ： That would certainly help us tremendously.

那將對我們幫助很大。

卡　特 ： Yes, indeed. 是的，的確如此。

HINT BANK ───────────────

• rush〔rʌʃ〕*adj.* 緊急的；急迫的　　manage〔ˈmænɪdʒ〕*v.* 設法做～；處理
• urgent〔ˈɝdʒənt〕*adj.* 緊急的　tremendously〔trɪˈmɛndəslɪ〕*adv.*〔俗〕非常地

✲ " fill that order " 句中的" fill "原意是指「填滿；充滿」的意思，在此是指「接受」的意思。

中國人1 ： Was there anything else you wished to discuss？

還有其他你想討論的嗎？

貝克爾 ： No, I think that's all.　Can you think of anything

else, John？

不，我想就是這些了。約翰，你想還有別的事嗎？

卡　特 ： No, *I don't believe so.* 不，我想沒有了。

HINT BANK ────────────────────

＊" I don't believe so. "是指" I believe I can't think of anything else. "

（我想沒有其他的事了。）

第 4 週

談話內容的敍述

4th Week — Hints on How to Express Various Concepts

◢Fourth Week, First Day◣

How to Express Obligation and Necessity

第四週，第一天 如何表達責任與需要

▶ BASIC DIALOGUES ◀

1. A : I ***must be*** at Betty's house by 3 o'clock.
　　 我必須在三點以前到貝蒂家。

B : Really? It's already 2:30. You'd better hurry.
　　 眞的嗎？已經二點半了，你最好快點。

2. A : Must you go so soon? 你必須這麼快走嗎？

B : Yes, I have an appointment at five.
　　 是的。我五點有個約會。

3. A : I ***had to*** write more than 10 letters this morning.
　　 今天早上我得寫十幾封信。

B : My, that was a lot of work, wasn't it?
　　 哇，很多工作，不是嗎？

4. A : We ***ought to*** leave early tomorrow morning.
　　 我們明天一早必須離開。

B : Yeah. We are supposed to be there at 8 o'clock.
　　是啊！我們八點要到那裏。

5. A : You **should** put part of your salary in the bank each month. 你每個月應該把一部分薪水存入銀行。

　　B : I'd like to, but I spend it all every month.
　　　我是想這麼做，但我每個月都把它花光。

6. A : You must study harder. 你必須更用功讀書。

　　B : Thank you for your advice. 謝謝你的勸告。

7. A : **It's absolutely necessary for** you to get a driver's license if you want to buy a car.
　　　你想買車的話，一定得先考一張駕駛執照。

　　B : I know. That's why I am taking lessons at a driving school.
　　　我知道，那就是我在一所駕駛訓練班上課的原因。

HINT BANK————————————————

・appointment〔ə'pɔɪntmənt〕*n.* 約會
・absolutely〔'æbsə,lutlɪ, ,æbsə'lutlɪ〕*adv.* 絕對地；完全地
・**driver's license** 駕駛執照　　**take lessons** 受課；學習（ = *have lessons* ）

＊表示義務、必須、當然的用詞有："must"，"ought to~"，"should"等等。

✕ APPLIED CONVERSATION ✕ 約會遲到

Being Unable to Keep an Appointment on Time

(Telephone bell rings. Receiver picked
up /電話響了，聽筒被拿起) --------

海　倫：Hello. 喂。

中國人：Hello, Helen. This is Mary.
I'm sorry but I can't leave
the office yet. 喂，海倫，我是
瑪麗。很抱歉，我還不能下班。

海　倫：What's the problem? 有什麼問題嗎？

中國人：Well, I have some things I ought to do before I leave.
呃，下班前我還有一些事情必須做。

海　倫：*Can't you leave it till tomorrow*? 不能明天再做嗎？

中國人：I'm afraid not. I'm a little behind in my work and I
feel it's my duty to get it done.
恐怕不行。我的工作進度有點落後，我想我有責任把它做完。

海　倫：Well, if it's something that must be done, I don't suppose you can ignore it.
如果眞的有事情要做，我想你不會把它丟在一邊。

中國人：No, *sloppy work's just not my bag.*
對，工作草率不是我的作風。

HINT BANK──────────────

· ignore〔ɪgˊnor, -ˊnɔr〕v. 不理睬；忽視　　sloppy〔ˊslɑpɪ〕adj. 草率的

＊ "What's the problem?" 是問「有什麼問題？」或「發生什麼事？」所以也可
以用 "What's the matter (with you)?" 來問對方。

海　倫： Sally is here with me. Suppose we go on ahead. You can come afterwards as soon as you've finished your work. Will that be all right?
莎莉現在和我在一起，我想我們先走，你一做完工作就來，這樣好嗎？

中國人： Yes, of course. I'm terribly sorry, but I feel responsible for the work and my boss is depending on me.
當然好。我眞的很抱歉，但我覺得必須負責把工作做好，而且老闆又信任我。

海　倫： We understand. But step on it, will you?
我們了解。但是儘快趕來，好嗎？

中國人： Oh, sure. It shouldn't take more than an hour to get this work done.
喔，當然。大概不到一小時就可以把這工作完成。

海　倫： Good. We'll see you over there. 好極了。我們在那裡碰面。
（ Sound of receiver being replaced /聽筒放回的聲音 ）-----------

海　倫： Mary says she still has some work to do and that she'll join us later at Joan's house.
瑪麗說她還有些工作要做，待會兒會在瓊那裡和我們會合。

莎　莉： *She's a real workaholic, isn't she*?
她眞是個工作狂，不是嗎？

HINT BANK────────────

· workaholic〔͵wɔkə'hɑlɪk〕*n.* 視人生即工作的人；工作狂（是由work和alcoholic所構成）

＊“ Step on it, will you?” 句中的“ step on it ”是「快一點」的意思。在命令句之後加“ will you ”可以緩和語氣。

＊“ It shouldn't take more than an hour.” 句中的“ should ”是表示自己的判斷。

海　倫：She certainly is. I suppose that's why her boss depends so much on her. He gives her complete responsibility over the operation of that office.

的確，我想那就是她老闆那麼信任她的原因，他把公司的營運交給她全權負責。

莎　莉：*She must have a lot on the ball*. 她一定很有才幹。

海　倫：Well, shall we leave? We promised to be there at 3 o'clock. It's already quarter to three.

我們該走了吧？我們答應三點要到那裡,現在差十五分就三點了。

莎　莉：Yes, I guess we'd better hurry. It will take a good fifteen minutes to get there.

嗯，我想我們得快點，到那裡足足要花十五分鐘。

海　倫：Will you see if the back door is locked?

請看看後門鎖好沒有？

莎　莉：It is. I locked it myself just a few minutes ago.

鎖好了。幾分鐘前我才鎖上的。

海　倫：Good. Let's go. 好，走吧！

HINT BANK ————————————

· *have a lot on the ball* 〔俗〕非常有才幹

＊ " a good fifteen minutes " 句中的 " good " 是指「充分；足夠」的意思。

＊ " Will you see if～? " 句中的 " see " 是指「檢查看看；確定一下」的意思。

Grammar and Usage

表示「義務」和「必要性」的說法有很多。現將其歸納如下：

1. *must* 和 *must not*

表示「必須」的意思，最常用到的是 "must"。這是表達「必要」的意思。

· I *must* go to her house.（我必須去她家。）

"must" 的否定句是用 "must not"，表示「不可」的禁止意思。若是要表達「沒有必要」，則用 "*need not*" 或 "*don't have to*"。

2. *have to*（= *have got to*）

在會話中，較常用 "have to" 來代替 "must"。分別用 "had to"、"will（shall）have to"、"have had to" 表示過去式、未來式及完成式的「必須」。

在口語用法中，可以用 "*have got to*"（或只用 "*got to*"），雖然形式上是過去式，但是，意思和用 "have to" 一樣。

3. *should* 和 *ought to*

"should" 和 "must" 相比較，「義務」的感覺較強。所以，一般都譯成「應該～」。例：

· You should be loyal to your country.（你應該為國盡忠。）

"*ought to*" 的用法和 "should" 相同。

4. 其他用法

表示「應該」的用法，還可用 "*It is one's duty to ～.*" 但是這種用法較正式又嚴肅，所以，通常前面會加 "I think" 或 "I feel" 來緩和語氣。

Fourth Week, Second Day

How to Voice Hopes or Expectations

第四週，第二天　如何表明希望或期望

BASIC DIALOGUES

1. A : I hope your play will be a great success.
　　　我希望你的演出很成功。

　B : Thank you very much. I hope so, too.
　　　非常謝謝你，我也希望如此。

2. A : *I hope to see you again real soon.*
　　　我希望很快能再看到你。

　B : So do I. 我也是。

3. A : I do hope you have a pleasant flight.
　　　我衷心希望你有個愉快的飛行。

　B : Thank you. I'll write to you as soon as I get back to the States. 謝謝。我一回到美國就會寫信給你。

4. A : It turned out exactly as we had hoped.
　　　結果正如我們所期望的。

　B : I'm glad to hear it. 我很高興聽到是這樣。

5. A : How did you do in your examinations? 你試考得怎樣？

B : Well, at least I answered all of the questions. I can only hope for the best.

哦，至少我回答了所有的問題。現在只能祈禱有好的結果。

6. A : I wish you every success in your new business.

祝你的新事業成功。

B : Thank you very much. I'm determined to try my best.

非常謝謝你。我決定盡我最大的努力去做。

7. A : *I expect great things of John in the near future.*

我期望不久的將來，約翰會有一番大作爲。

B : That's just what I was going to say. Everybody speaks very highly of him.

我正想說這句話。每個人都很稱讚他。

8. A : What time do you expect him back?

你想他何時會回來？

B : He said he'd be back by five. 他說五點前會回來。

9. A : *We're expecting to* see Mr. Jones at Jim's party to-morrow evening.

我們期待明晚在吉姆的宴會中，與瓊斯先生見面。

B : How nice. He will be very glad to see you both again.

真好！他將很高興再看到你們兩個。

HINT BANK ————————————————————

· *turn out* （結果）變成…   *at least* 至少

· *try one's best* 盡～最大的努力

* " I wish you every success." 句中的 " every " 是作爲加強語氣用。

▶◀ APPLIED CONVERSATION ▶◀ 到飛機場為美國朋友送行

Seeing American Friends off at the Airport

史密斯先生 : Well, Mr. Lee, it certainly
was nice of you and your wife
to come and see us off.
李先生，你和尊夫人來給我
們送行，真是親切。

中國人1 : Not at all, Mr. Smith. We
certainly hope you had a
nice time during your stay
in Taiwan.
那兒的話，史密斯先生，我們真的希望你們在台灣停留
期間玩得很愉快。

史密斯先生 : Indeed we did, Mr. Lee. You and Mrs. Lee were so
kind to us. We appreciate it very much.
我們的確玩得很愉快，李先生。你和尊夫人對我們這麼
親切，我們非常感激。

中國人1 : *We were able to do so little*. We do hope you'll be
able to come back to Taiwan for a longer stay.
我們所做的不過一點點。我們真希望你們能再到台灣來，
停留久一點。

HINT BANK —————————————————————————

· *see ~ off* 送行；送別

史密斯先生 : Well, we hope we'll have a chance to come back
again. 哦，我們希望有機會再來。

中國人1 : I know that all of my friends would agree.
我相信我所有的朋友都希望如此。

史密斯先生 : It's very kind of you to say that. Incidentally, do you
expect *you'll ever have a chance to visit America*?
謝謝你這麼說。順便一提，你希望有機會到美國一遊嗎？

中國人1 : Well, there is always the chance that I may go
there. You see, we have a branch office in New York.
唔，我一直有去那裏的機會。你知道，我們在紐約有分
公司。

史密斯太太 : It's quite lovely in New York at this time of the
year. I do hope Mrs. Lee will be able to accompany
you if you do have the chance to come.
紐約每年這個時候都很迷人，我真希望如果你有機會來
的話，李夫人能陪你一起來。

中國人1 : If my company will permit it, I hope to take my
wife. 如果公司批准，我希望帶我太太一起去。

史密斯先生 : Did you go with your husband, Mrs. Lee, when he
made the trip to India?
李太太，你先生去印度時，你也去了嗎？

HINT BANK

• accompany〔əˈkʌmpənɪ〕*v*. 陪伴

中國人2 : No, I wasn't able to go. You see, *I was expecting my baby* at that time.

　　　　　　沒有，我無法去。你知道，那時候我正懷著寶寶。

史密斯太太 : You have our New York address, don't you? You must write to us.

　　　　　　你有我們紐約的地址，不是嗎？你一定要寫信給我們。

中國人2 : I shall indeed. 我一定會。

中國人1 : I think I heard your flight number called. You'd better get going.

　　　　　　我想我聽到登機的廣播了，你們最好動身吧。

史密斯先生 : Well, thank you again for coming.

　　　　　　再一次謝謝你們來送行。

中國人1 : Not at all, Mr. Smith. We both hope you have a nice flight home.

　　　　　　不客氣，史密斯先生。我們倆祝你們回家的旅途愉快。

史密斯先生 : Thank you. I know we shall. And *please give our very best regards to* all of our mutual friends.

　　　　　　謝謝，我們會的。請代我們問候所有我們共同的朋友。

HINT BANK ─────────────────────

* mutual 〔ˈmjutʃuəl〕*adj.* 共同的

* " be expecting ～ "這是表示「懷孕」的口語用法。注意要用進行式。

* 祝福要搭飛機的人「旅途愉快」是用 " I hope you have a nice flight." 如果對方要搭船，就用 " I hope you have a nice voyage."（祝你一帆風順。）

中國人1 ： Of course. Goodbye, Mrs. Smith, and do come back
　　　　　to Taiwan again.

　　　　　　沒問題。再見，史密斯太太，一定要再來台灣哦！

史密斯太太 ： Goodbye, and don't forget to come to New York

　　　　　　再見，別忘了到紐約來。

中國人2 ： Goodbye.　再見。

史密斯先生 ： Goodbye.　再見。

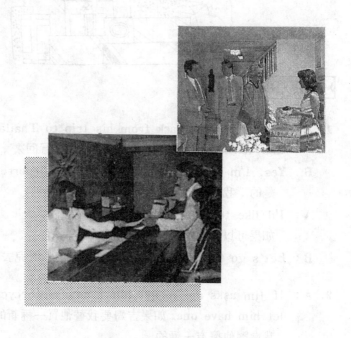

▐ Fourth Week, Third Day ▐

How to Voice Intention or Plans

第四週，第三天　如何表明意願或打算

▶ BASIC DIALOGUES ◀

1. A : Tom is coming back from his trip to Thailand this even-
        ing, isn't he？湯姆今天下午從泰國旅行回來，不是嗎？

   B : Yes. I'm going to meet him at the airport.
       是的，我要去機場接他。

   A : I'd like to go with you if I may.
       如果可以的話，我想跟你一道去。

   B : Let's go together, then. 那麼，我們一塊兒去。

2. A : If Jim asks me to get him a new motorcycle, I will
        let him have one. 如果吉姆要我替他買一輛新的摩托車的話，
        我會讓他擁有一輛的。

   B : I don't think he will ask you to. I suppose he wants to
       have a car. 我想他不會要你替他買一輛摩托車。我認為，他
       想要有一輛汽車。

3. A: *I'm thinking of* making a trip to Australia during the summer vacation. 我想在暑假時，到澳洲旅行。

B: Wonderful. I'm sure you'll enjoy your trip very much.
好極了，我確信你的旅行一定很愉快。

4. A: *We're planning* to give you a farewell party. What day would be most convenient for you?
我們正計劃要替你辦一個歡送會。對你來說，哪一天最方便呢?

B: Well, that's very kind of you. Saturday next week would be most convenient for me.
嗯，你們真是親切。下星期六對我來說最方便。

5. A: I've arranged to invite all our colleagues to the party.
我已經安排好，要邀請我們所有的同事參加這個宴會。

B: Fine. I'm looking forward to seeing all the familiar faces. 很好，我盼望見到所有熟悉的面孔。

HINT BANK ────────────────

· get〔gɛt〕v. 買（ = buy ）   *farewell party* 歡送會（=*farewell meeting*）

✱ 請注意「下禮拜六」是用 " Saturday next week " 而不是用 " next Saturday"。

◀ APPLIED CONVERSATION ▶ 計劃到南台灣旅行

Planning a Trip to Southern Taiwan

約　翰：Good morning, Mei-mei. I
came over this morning to
discuss our trip through
southern Taiwan. 早安，美
美。我今天早上過來討論我
們到南台灣旅行的事。

中國人：*What a coincidence* ! Lily
and I were discussing the
trip last night and she has worked out a rough schedule
for the trip.
多巧啊！莉莉和我昨天正討論到這次旅行，而且她已經周密
地擬定這次旅行的大概行程。

莉　莉：John, do you think one week will be too long for the
entire trip？約翰，你想這整個旅程，一週會不會太長？

約　翰：Well, I'd planned to be gone for only five days, but I
guess I can extend it a couple of days.
嗯，我計劃只去五天，不過我想，我可以延個幾天。

中國人：Good！*According to the schedule we worked out*,
we'll leave Taipei on Sunday night and return the fol-
lowing Saturday.
很好！根據我們擬定的計劃，我們將在星期天晚上離開台北，
第二個星期六回來。

HINT BANK————————————————

- coincidence〔ko'ɪnsədəns〕*n*. 巧合　　*work out* 周密地擬定
- rough〔rʌf〕*adj*. 概略的

約　翰： Do your plans call for a visit to Coral Lake?
你們的計劃有沒有要去珊瑚潭玩？

中國人： Well, Coral Lake isn't on our present schedule, but we could work in if you like. 嗯，珊瑚潭不在我們現在的計劃上，不過，如果你喜歡的話，我們可以把它插進去。

約　翰： Oh, I've just got to see Coral Lake. I understand it's one of the most beautiful places in all Taiwan.
喔，我一定要去看珊瑚潭。我知道它是全台灣最美的地方之一。

莉　莉： Well, we could stop off at Coral Lake if we don't stay overnight at Tainan County. 嗯，如果我們不在台南縣過夜的話，就可以在珊瑚潭稍作逗留。

中國人： Don't you think we could do The South Kunshen Temple and Kuantzeling Hot Springs in one day? 你們不認為，我們可以在一天之內，去南鯤鯓廟和關子嶺溫泉嗎？

莉　莉： Well, the schedule will be pretty tight, but we could do it. 嗯，時間表將會十分緊湊，不過我們可以這麼做。

約　翰： If it's possible, let's do that and put Coral Lake on our schedule. 如果可能的話，我們就這麼做，而且把珊瑚潭放進我們的計劃中。

莉　莉： All right, I'll work it out. 好的，我會把它擬定出來。

HINT BANK ────────────────────

· **work in** 插入　　coral〔'kɑrəl〕*n.* 珊瑚
· **stop off** 稍事逗留；作短時間停留而在中途下車

* "I've just got to see~." 用 "have got to" 和用 "have to" 一樣，都是表示「一定要」的意思，而 "just" 在此是加強語氣的作用。

中國人： Is there some other place you wish to visit particularly？ 還有沒有哪些地方，你特別想去玩的？

約　翰： No, *not that I can think of at the moment*.
　　　　 沒有，現在我還想不出來。

莉　莉： According to the schedule I've worked out, we'll be travelling mostly at night. That will leave the daylight hours for sightseeing.
　　　　 根據我擬定出來的計劃，我們大部分是晚上旅行，這樣白天的時間就可以觀光了。

約　翰： That's a good idea, but do you think we'll be able to get seat reservations？
　　　　 這是個好主意，不過，你想我們可以預訂得到座位嗎？

中國人： Well, we still have more than two weeks, so I think we'll be able to make reservations.
　　　　 嗯，我們還有兩個多禮拜，所以我想我們可以預約。

約　翰： And have you planned on what inns we'll be staying at？
　　　　 還有，你們是否有計劃我們要住什麼旅館？

HINT BANK ─────────────────────

· *at the moment* 現在　　 sightseeing〔'saɪt,siɪŋ〕n. 觀光；遊覽
· inn〔ɪn〕n. 旅館；客棧（通常指比 *hotel* 小而又老式的）

＊ " not that I can think of at the moment " 是指 " there is not any place that I can think of at the moment "（現在我想不出任何地方來）。

莉 莉： Yes, I've made a list of inns at the various places we'll stop, but as I said before, we'll be travelling mostly at night.

是的，我已經列好一張我們在各個不同地方停留的旅館名單，不過，就像我以前說過的，我們大部分是在晚上旅行。

約 翰： That will save us quite a bit of money, won't it ?

那會省掉我們很多錢，不是嗎？

莉 莉： Yes, *that's one of the reasons* I planned it this way.

是的，這就是為什麼我會這樣計劃的理由之一。

▶ Fourth Week, Fourth Day ◀

How to Voice Conjecture or Surmise

第四週，第四天　如何說明推測

⊳ **BASIC DIALOGUES** ◁

1. A : May I see Mr. Wilson？ 我可以見威爾遜先生嗎？

   B : I'm sorry, he's in conference now. *I think* the conference will be finished in half an hour. Will you wait,
sir？ 抱歉，他現在在開會。我想會議在半個小時內就會結束。
先生，請你稍等好嗎？

   A : Yes, of course. 好的，當然。

2. A : *I guess* Mr. Wilson will be very busy this afternoon.
我想威爾遜先生今天下午會很忙。

   B : Yes. He is scheduled to attend a cocktail party at two,
and has another appointment for four thirty.
是的，他預定兩點參加雞尾酒會，四點半還有另外一個約會。

3. A : *Do you suppose* Mr. Thomas will return to the office
by three？ 你想，湯瑪斯先生下午三點以前會回到辦公室嗎？

B： I doubt if he will be back before four.

我懷疑四點以前他是否會回來。

4. **A**： I imagine the traffic is very congested at this time of day. You'd better stay here a little longer.

我想，一天當中的這個時候，交通非常擁擠，你最好是在這裏留久一點。

B： Thanks. That's a good idea. 謝謝，這是個好主意。

5. **A**： *He must be caught in the traffic.* 他一定是被交通所阻。

B： I guess so, too. The traffic is terrific these days, isn't it? 我想也是，這幾天交通真是可怕，不是嗎？

6. **A**： The sky is overcast. It'll probably begin to rain soon.

天氣很陰暗，可能很快就要開始下雨了。

B： I'm afraid the rain will change to storm before evening.

恐怕雨在傍晚以前，就會變成暴風雨。

HINT BANK——————————

· *be in conference* 正在舉行會議（= *hold a conference*）

· *be scheduled to* 預定

· *cocktail party* 雞尾酒會（通常在下午舉行的社交聚會、喝雞尾酒及吃各種點心類）

· congest〔kənˈdʒɛst〕*v.* 使擁塞；使充滿

· terrific〔təˈrɪfɪk〕*adj.* 可怕的；猛烈的

· overcast〔ˈovəˌkæst〕*adj.* 陰天的；陰暗的

＊ "will be finished" 是指「將結束」，通常都是用被動式，不用 "will finish"。

◀ APPLIED CONVERSATION ▶ 等待友人到達

Waiting for Friends to Arrive

湯　姆：Hello, David. Aren't Betty
　　　　and Mei-mei here yet?
　　　　嗨，大衞，貝蒂和美美還沒有
　　　　到這裏嗎？

中國人1：No, they haven't come yet,
　　　　but I guess they'll be here
　　　　shortly.
　　　　不，她們還沒有到，不過我想
　　　　她們不久就會到了。

湯　姆：Did you tell them three o'clock sharp?
　　　　你告訴過她們是三點正嗎？

中國人1：Yes, three o'clock at the information counter at Taipei
　　　　Station. 是的，三點鐘在台北火車站服務台。

湯　姆：Well, I suppose they'll be here soon. After all there's
　　　　still 30 minutes before train time. 嗯，我想她們很快就
　　　　會到這裏了。畢竟離火車開車時間，還有三十分鐘。

中國人1：*It's just a guess*, but maybe they stopped off to do
　　　　some last-minute shopping. You know how girls are.
　　　　只是猜想而已，不過也許她們中途停留，在最後幾分鐘買東
　　　　西。你知道女孩是怎樣的。

HINT BANK

- shortly〔'ʃɔrtlɪ〕*adv.* 不久；即刻　　　*stop off*〔俗〕中途停留片刻

湯　姆： I suppose you're right.　You don't think they've got the wrong day, do you?

我想你是對的。你想她們不會是弄錯日期了吧，不是嗎？

中國人1： I don't think that's possible.　You see, I told Betty and Mei-mei separately.

我想那是不可能的。你知道的，我分別告訴過貝蒂和美美。

湯　姆： I wonder if they're coming together.

不知道他們是不是一起來的。

中國人1： It was my impression they were coming together.

我的印象中，她們是一起來的。

湯　姆： Well, I guess we've just got to wait here.

嗯，我想我們只有在這裏等了。

中國人1： Yes, I suppose so.　Say, will you watch these bags while I go over to that stand to buy some cigarettes?

是的，我想是的。喂，我到那個攤子買香煙時，請你看這些袋子好嗎？

湯　姆： Sure, David. 當然，大衛。

貝　蒂： Hi, Tom.　Are we late? 嗨，湯姆，我們遲到了嗎？

中國人2： We didn't keep you waiting, did we?　Where's David?

我們沒讓你等，不是嗎？大衛在哪裏？

HINT BANK——————————

· separately〔'sɛpərɪtlɪ〕adv. 各別地　　stand〔stænd〕n. 攤子；攤位

* "We've just got to wait here." 句中用 " have got to " 和 " have to " 的意思相同。

湯　姆　: Well, *so you finally turned up*. David is over there at that stand buying some cigarettes. Here he comes.

　　　　　嗯，你們終於出現了。大衛在那邊那個攤子買些煙。他來了。

貝　蒂　: Hello, David. I guess we're a little late.

　　　　　嗨，大衛，我想我們有點遲到了。

中國人₁ : Well, we're glad you got here. We were beginning to think all sorts of bad thoughts.

　　　　　嗯，我們很高興，你們到了。我們開始有各種不好的想法。

貝　蒂　: *Like what*？譬如什麼？

湯　姆　: Oh, like one of you getting appendicitis or getting hit by a truck. Isn't that right, David？

　　　　　喔，像是你們當中有一個人得了盲腸炎，或是給大卡車撞了。對不對，大衛？

中國人₁ : Yes, you're right. 是的，你說得對。

中國人₂ : Oh, don't be silly. We got here in plenty of time and you shouldn't complain.

　　　　　喔，別傻了。我們到達這裏有充分的時間，你們不應該抱怨。

湯　姆　: No, I guess we shouldn't. I think the train is already in. *Shall we be going*？

　　　　　不，我想我們不應該。我想火車已經進站了。我們該走了嗎？

中國人₁ : Yes, let's go. Do you have the tickets, Tom？

　　　　　是的，我們走吧，湯姆，你有票嗎？

湯　姆　: Yes, I have them here. 是的，票在這裏。

HINT BANK─────────

・ appendicitis〔ə,pɛndə'saɪtɪs〕*n*.〔醫〕盲腸炎　*in plenty of time* 有充分的時間

⟨═ Grammar and Usage ═⟩

1. 「推測」的句型及用法

"I think ～ .", "I guess ～ .", "I suppose ～ ."和"I imagine ～ ."這些句型可以用在表示*純粹的*推測，也可用在使措辭委婉而附加的用法上。用在會話中，大部分是用這些句型使語氣委婉一點。例如："It's too expensive."（這個價錢太貴。）聽起來有責備的感覺。但是，如果用"I *think* it's too expensive."（我想這個價錢太貴。）語氣聽起來較溫和。

2. 和 *I think ～* . 類似的用法

在英文中，有「想」的意思的字彙有"think"，"suppose"，"guess"，"imagine"等等，其中使用最頻繁的是"think"。

"guess"本來是「推測」的意思，"suppose"和"imagine"本來也是「想像」的意思。但是在會話中，幾乎和"think"的意思相同。

其他還有較嚴肅的說法，如：

- I *consider* it to be right to do so.
  （我認為這樣做是對的。）
- I *gather* your opinion is well justified.
  （我想你的意見是正確的。）
- I *presume* you're Mr. Smith, aren't you?
  （我想你是史密斯先生，不是嗎？）

3. 以助動詞表示「推測」的用法

在助動詞中，可以表示「推測」意思的有："must"，"may"，"will"等。用"must"是「必定…」，用在有相當把握時。而"may"和"might"是「也許～」，把握的程度較輕。

Fourth Week, Fifth Day

How to Express Concession, Condition or Supposition

第四週，第五天　如何表達讓步、條件或假設

BASIC DIALOGUES

1. **A :** I know it's a good camera, but the price is a little too high. 我知道這台相機很好，但是價格有點太貴了。。

   B : If that's the case, we'd like to recommend our installment system.

   　　如果情形是這樣的話，我們想推薦分期付款的辦法。

2. **A :** *What do you think of this dress* ? 你認為這件衣服如何？

   B : Well, I don't like the color or the material, though the style is very good.

   　　嗯，我不喜歡這個顏色或者這種質料，雖然款式很好。

3. **A :** If I had more money with me now, I would buy these shoes. 如果我現在身邊有更多錢的話，我會買這些鞋的。

   B : I can lend you some if you can return the money by tomorrow evening.

   　　如果你可以在明天下午還錢的話，我可以借你一些。

4. A : Suppose I gave you 10,000 dollars, what would you like to buy with it？假設我給你一萬塊的話，你想拿來買什麼？

B : I'd like to buy a telescope. 我想買一台望遠鏡。

5. A : I'd like to ask for your permission to use a passage from your book in the essay I'm now writing.

　　我想徵求你的同意，在我現在寫的論文中用你書裏面的一段。

B : Well, I can give you permission to use any passage on condition that you mention in your essay the title of the book from which the passage is taken.

　　嗯，我可以允許你用任何一段，如果你在論文中提及這一段出處的書名。

HINT BANK───────────

- installment〔ɪn'stɔlmənt〕*n.* 分期付款
- telescope〔'tɛlə,skop〕*n.* 望遠鏡　　***ask for*** 要求；請求
- passage〔'pæsɪdʒ〕*n.*（引用文句等的）一節；一段
- ***on condition that*** 在～的條件下；若～則

* "If I had more money with me now, ～ ." 這是與「現在事實相反的假設」。實際上「現在沒有更多的錢」。

* " suppose " 用在假設語句中，用法、意思都和 " if " 相同。

◄ APPLIED CONVERSATION ► 進行交易

A Business Transaction

外國人： Good afternoon, Mr. Lin.
午安，林先生。

中國人： Good afternoon, Mr. Benson.
It was kind of you to come
and see me. I asked you to
drop in so we could discuss
the proposal I made to you
over the telephone.

午安，班森先生。你來看我眞是親切。我請你來，這樣我們可
以討論我在電話中對你所提的案子。

外國人： Yes, certainly. 是的，當然。

中國人： *I believe I mentioned* the figure of 40 million dollars
as the price for the property. Is that satisfactory
with you ?
我相信我提過那筆地產的價格是四千萬這個數目。這對你來
說滿意嗎？

HINT BANK───────────────

- proposal 〔prə'pozl〕 *n.* 提案；提議
- property 〔'prɑpətɪ〕 *n.* 地產 (= *estate*)
- satisfactory 〔,sætɪs'fæktərɪ〕 *adj.* 令人滿意的

＊ " so we would ～" 這是口語用法。寫文章時，通常用 " so that we could～"。

外國人： To tell you the truth, Mr. Lin, the location of the property isn't exactly *what I had in mind*. Of course the location isn't bad, but I would have preferred a corner lot.

說老實話，林先生，這筆地產的地點，不完全是我心裏所想（要）的。當然地點不壞，不過我比較喜歡拐角的土地。

中國人： I see. 我知道了。

外國人： Of course, if you could reduce the price, I might consider buying it.

當然，如果你可以降低價格的話，我可以考慮買下它。

中國人： Well, that might be arranged, but I would have to discuss it with my client. How much of a reduction would you want?

嗯，這可以商量，不過我必須和我的委託人討論。你希望減多少價？

外國人： I might consider it if you reduced the price by five million.

如果你減五百萬，我會考慮的。

中國人： That would be quite a reduction, wouldn't it? I'm afraid my client might not agree. *How about meeting me halfway* — a reduction of 2,500,000 dollars?

那減的相當多，不是嗎？恐怕我的委託人不會同意。跟我妥協一下如何——減兩百五十萬元。

HINT BANK

• *not exactly* 不完全是；未必　　*have in mind* 計劃；欲
• client〔'klaɪənt〕*n.* 委託人；客戶　　*meet sb. halfway* 跟人妥協

外國人：Well, I'd like to reconsider before I give you a definite answer. Will that be all right?

嗯，在我給你明確答案以前，我想再考慮一下。可以嗎？

中國人：Of course. And in the meantime, I will speak with my client.

當然。同時，我要和我的委託人談。

外國人：Incidentally, are there any other conditions with regard to the purchase of this property?

順便一提，關於購買這筆地產，有沒有其他條件？

中國人：My client insists on one condition.

我的委託人堅持一個條件。

外國人：May I ask what it is? 我可以問問是什麼嗎？

中國人：Yes. My client will not sell the land if the structure to be built on the land is an apartment house.

是的，如果建在這塊土地上的建築物是公寓房子的話，我的委託人不會賣這塊土地。

外國人：*There will be no difficulty there*. You see, I intend to build my own residence there.

這沒有什麼難的。你知道，我想在那裏建自己的住宅。

中國人：I understand. Now, if my client will agree to the price of 37,500,000 dollars, I'm sure we can conclude this deal.

我了解。那麼，如果我的委託人同意三千七百五十萬元的價格，我確信我們就可以締結這個交易了。

HINT BANK

- definite〔'dɛfənɪt〕 *adj*. 明確的   *with regard to* 有關～；關於～
- structure〔'strʌktʃə〕 *n*. 建築物；構造   residence〔'rɛzədəns〕 *n*. 住宅
- conclude〔kən'klud〕 *v*. 締結（ = *settle* ）訂立

外國人： Yes, but I myself would like a little more time to reconsider the $ 37,500,000 price.

是的，不過我自己想要多一點時間，再考慮一下三千七百五十萬的價格。

中國人： Of course. Suppose I call you next Monday and give you my client's definite answer.

當然。我下星期一打電話給你，告訴你我的委託人明確的回覆如何。

外國人： Fine, Mr. Lin. And I'm sure I shall have reached a decision by that time, too.

很好，林先生。我確信到那個時候，我也會有個決定。

HINT BANK

- suppose〔sə'poz〕*v.* ～吧；～如何（用於祈使句中，引出一項建議）

- ***reach a decision*** 獲致解決；決定（＝*arrive at a decision ＝ come to a decision*）

- ＊" I shall have reached a decision." 這是未來完成式，表示「到未來某時之前，已經～」之意。

Fourth Week, Sixth Day

Hints on How to Link or Continue a Conversation

第四週，第六天　如何連接或繼續對話

BASIC DIALOGUES

1. A : Please have a seat and make yourself comfortable.

請坐，不要拘束。

B : Thank you. ***Incidentally***, when did you return from your trip to South Africa?

謝謝。順便問一下，你什麼時候從南非之旅回來？

A : Two weeks ago. 兩個禮拜以前。

2. B : Please have a cup of tea. I know you prefer tea to coffee. 請喝杯茶。我知道你比較喜歡茶，而不喜歡咖啡。

A : Yes, thanks. ***By the way***, I saw a very good pipe at Tonlin Department Store the other day.

是的，謝謝。順便一提，我前幾天在統領百貨看到一支很好的煙斗。

B : Oh, did you? What was the price? 喔，是嗎？多少錢？

A : Eight thousand dollars. Of course it's an imported pipe. 八千元。當然那是一支進口的煙斗。

3. A : I think I'd better be running along now. I have an
appointment for three o'clock.

我想，我最好是現在就出發，三點鐘我有個約會。

B : That reminds me. *To tell the truth*, I have an appointment myself for three. Let's go togther part of the
way if we are going in the same direction.

這提醒了我，老實說，我自己三點鐘也有個約會。如果是要
去同一個方向的話，我們就一起走一段。

4. A : Long time no see. How have you been?

很久不見。最近好嗎？

B : I've been real well. As a matter of fact, my wife and
I are expecting our first child.

好極了。事實上，我和我太太快有我們第一個的孩子。

A : Oh! Congratulations! I'm so happy for both of you.

喔！恭喜！恭喜！我眞替你們感到高興。

HINT BANK ───────────────

· *run along* 出發；走

* 在對話中，如果要轉變話題，或者敍述和前面沒有直接關係的事時可以用 " incidentally " 或 " by the way "。

⟩⟨ APPLIED CONVERSATION ⟩⟨ 邀朋友看電影

Taking Friends to the Movies

蘇　珊：Oh, hello, Martha. ***How nice
of you to drop in!***

　　　　喔，嗨，瑪莎，你來眞好！

中國人：Hello, Susan. I hadn't seen
you for such a long time that
I thought I'd just drop in for
a little chat.

　　　　嗨，蘇珊，我好久沒看到你了，
所以想來聊聊天。

蘇　珊：I'm so glad you did. By the way, you can stay for
dinner, can't you?

　　　　你來聊天我眞高興。順便一提，你可以留下來吃晚飯，不
是嗎？

中國人：But it would be so much bother for you.

　　　　不過這會太麻煩你了。

蘇　珊：Indeed not. No bother at all. 眞的不會，一點也不麻煩。

中國人：By the way, when does Fred get back from the office?

　　　　順便問一下，弗瑞德什麼時候從辦公室回來？

HINT BANK────────────────

- chat〔tʃæt〕*n.* 閒聊；聊天（＝*gossip*)　 bother〔'baðɚ〕*n.* 麻煩；煩心

* " How nice of you to ~." 是 " It's nice of you to ~." 的感嘆句。

* " Indeed not." 句中的 " not" 是否定前面 " It's would be so much bother
for you." 的句子。

蘇　珊：Let me see... He should be back in an hour or so. That reminds me. I'd better call him up and tell him not to be late for dinner.

　　　　讓我想想看…他應該在大約一個小時之後會回來。這提醒了我，我最好是打電話告訴他不要晚回來吃飯。

中國人：How about going to the movies after dinner? I'll treat.

　　　　晚飯後去看電影如何？我請客。

蘇　珊：That's a good idea, but we'll make Fred pay. You know he just got his bonus.

　　　　這是個好主意，不過我們讓弗瑞德付錢。你知道他剛拿到紅利。

中國人：As a matter of fact I just got mine. *That's why* I wanted to treat you two.

　　　　實際上我剛拿到我的（紅利）。這就是爲什麼我要請你們兩位。

蘇　珊：Well, I guess I'm the only one that isn't qualified to pay for the movies.

　　　　嗯，我想我是唯一沒有資格付電影錢的人。

中國人：*How right you are!* 你說得對極了！

HINT BANK ─────────────────

· bonus〔'bonəs〕*n.* 紅利　　　*as a matter of fact* 實際上

＊ "I just got mine." 句中的 "mine" 是指 "my bonus"。

蘇 珊：By the way, how is your mother？
順便問一下，你的母親好嗎？

中國人：Oh, she's quite well. She's staying at my uncle's place for a few days. That's why I don't have to be home for dinner.
喔，她相當好，她在我叔叔家住幾天。這就是為什麼我不必回家吃晚餐。

蘇 珊：How nice. *Will you excuse me a minute*？I'll call Fred.
眞好。我離開一會兒好嗎？我打電話給弗瑞德。

（ Sound of telephone dialing ╱ 撥電話的聲音 ）----------

蘇 珊：Fred? This is Susan. You won't be late for dinner, will you? Martha is here and we're going to have dinner together. She says she'll treat us to the movies later.
弗瑞德？我是蘇珊。你不會晚回來吃晚飯吧，不是嗎？瑪莎在這裏，我們要一塊兒吃晚飯。她說晚點要請我們去看電影。

弗瑞德：No, I'll be leaving the office in a few minutes. I'll see you later.
不會，我將在幾分鐘後離開辦公室。待會兒見。

蘇 珊：Fine. We'll be waiting. 很好，我們會等你。

（ Sound of receiver being replaced on cradle ╱ 話筒放回支架的聲音 ）------

---

HINT BANK

• cradle〔'kredḷ〕*n.*（電話聽筒的）支架

* "Will you excuse me a minute？" 這是表示要暫時離開座位時的用語。

中國人： Fred won't be late, will he? 弗瑞德不會晚回來，不是嗎？

蘇　珊： No, he says he's just leaving the office.
　　　　不會，他說他正要離開辦公室。

中國人： Can I help you with the dinner? 我可以幫你做晚飯嗎？

蘇　珊： Oh, that reminds me. I have the roast in the oven!...
　　　　喔，這提醒了我。烤箱裏面有烤肉！…

中國人： It isn't burned, is it? 沒有燒焦吧，不是嗎？

蘇　珊： No, thank goodness. It seems to be just right. As a
　　　　matter of fact *you reminded me just in time.*
　　　　沒有，感謝上帝。看起來似乎剛剛好，實際上，你提醒我提
　　　　醒得正是時候。

中國人： Do you mind if I play a record on the stereo?
　　　　我在立體音響上放張唱片，你不介意吧？

蘇　珊： Of course not. Go right ahead.
　　　　當然不會，請放。

HINT BANK ——————————————

• roast〔rost〕 *n.* 烤肉；紅燒肉　　stereo〔'stɛrɪo, 'stɪrɪo〕 *n.* 立體音響

＊ "Go right ahead." 是「請便；請不要客氣」的意思。"go ahead" 原是「做
　得順利」的意思。"right" 在此當加強語氣用。

與初見面的老外交談

5th Week   Conversations with Strangers

Fifth Week, First Day
Giving Directions
第五週，第一天 指 路

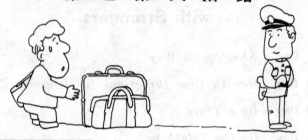

BASIC DIALOGUES

1. **A**: *Excuse me, but can you tell me where* the nearest post office is?

   對不起，不過可否請你告訴我，最近的郵局在哪裏？

   B: Certainly. Go straight until you come to a traffic light. Turn right there, and you'll find it on your right-hand side after walking for a few minutes.

   當然。直走到紅綠燈，在那裏右轉，再走幾分鐘你會發現郵局在你的右手邊。

2. **A**: *Pardon me, but could you direct me* to Taipei Station?

   對不起，不過你可否告訴我，台北火車站怎麼走？

   B: Of course. Go down this street and turn left at the second corner. Taipei Station is only two or three blocks down from the corner.

   當然。沿這條街走下去，在第二個街角的地方左轉。台北火車站就在離那個街角下去，祇有兩、三個街區的地方。

3. A : I beg your pardon, but could you tell me how to get to the Chiang kai-shek Memorial Hall ?

對不起，不過可否請你告訴我，怎麼到中正紀念堂？

B : Certainly. You can see a bus stop over there, can't you ? Take No. 294 or 36 there, and get off at Hang Chou S. Rd. The entrance to the Memorial Hall can be seen on the same side of the bus stop.

當然。你可以看到那邊的公車站，不是嗎？到那裏搭二九四路或三十六路，在杭州南路下車。就可以在公車站的同一邊，看到紀念堂的入口。

4. A : Excuse me. I'm looking for the home of a Mr. Lee. Do you know where he lives ?

對不起，我在找李先生的家，你知道他住哪裏嗎？

B : Fortunately, I live just next door to him. I'll go with you if you don't mind.

很幸運地，我就住在他的隔壁。如果你不介意的話，我跟你一塊兒走。

5. A : Excuse me, but can you tell me how I can get to the Far East Building ?

對不起，不過可否請你告訴我，怎麼到遠東大樓？

B : I'm very sorry, but I'm a total stranger around here myself. You'd better ask someone else.

很抱歉，我自己對這附近完全陌生，你最好問別人。

HINT BANK————————————————

· stranger〔'strendʒɚ〕*n.* 陌生人；異鄉人

· "Excuse me, but~?"和"Pardon me, but~?"都是客氣地向別人詢問事情的句型。

◖ APPLIED CONVERSATION ◗ 在派出所

At a Policebox

外國人 : Good afternoon. *I've just come to Taiwan* from the United States and dropped in to ask about directions to two places I want to see in Taipei.
午安，我剛從美國到台灣，
來問台北兩個我想去遊覽的地方該怎麼走。

警 察 : Of course, sir. Which are the places you wish to go to? 當然，先生。你希望去的地方是哪裏？

外國人 : Well, I want to go to the Chiang Kai-shek Memorial Hall, and I also wish to see the International House.
嗯，我想去中正紀念堂，而且我也希望去看國際學舍。

警 察 : *They are both within walking distance from here.*
這兩個地方，走路都可以到達。

外國人 : First, tell me how to get to the Chiang Kai-shek Memorial Hall.
首先，告訴我怎麼到中正紀念堂。

警 察 : Let me get you a map. It will be easier to explain.
我拿一張地圖給你，這樣比較容易解釋。

HINT BANK

· *police box* 派出所；值班崗亭（ = *police stand* ）

外國人：That's very nice of you. 你真好。

警　察：Let me see, er... this is where you are at the present time... in the Chengchung District.

　　　　我想想看，呃…這是你現在所在的位置…在城中區。

外國人：I see. 我明白了。

警　察：Now, this is Chinshan South Road. You go straight down this road for about five blocks until you come to Hsinyi Road Section 2.

　　　　嗯，這是金山南路。你沿這條路一直走，走大約五個街區，直到信義路二段。

外國人：Is Hsinyi Road easy to recognize?

　　　　信義路很容易認嗎？

警　察：Oh, yes. It is the first big intersection as you walk down Chinshan South Road.

　　　　喔，是的。你沿著金山南路往下走，遇到第一個大的十字路口就是信義路。

外國人：I see. And *Where do I go from there*?

　　　　我知道了。我到了那裏以後，應該怎麼走？

警　察：When you come to the intersection, turn to the right and go straight down that road. Chiang Kai-shek Memorial Hall will be on your left. It is a large blue-white building. 到了十字路口以後，往右轉，沿著那條路一直往下走，中正紀念堂就在你的左邊。它是一座藍白的建築物。

HINT BANK ─────────────────────────

・ *at the present time* 現在；現今　　recognize〔ˈrekəgˌnaɪz〕v. 辨認

外國人： I see. Now, how do I get to the International House?
我知道了。那現在我該怎樣去國際學舍？

警　察： I think the best way would be to take the same road
as you would to the Chiang Kai-shek Memorial Hall.
Only turn to the left, *instead of to the right*, at the
large intersection.
我想最好的辦法，就是走要到中正紀念堂的同一條路。只
是你到了大十字路口的時候，要左轉，而不是右轉。

外國人： Yes, and how do I go from there？
是的，到了那裏以後，我該怎麼走？

警　察： Go straight down that road until you come to Hsinsheng
South Road. There is a large intersection.
沿著那條路一直走下去，直到你到了新生南路為止，那裏
有一個大十字路口。

外國人： And from there？到了那裏以後呢？

警　察： You'll be able to see the International House diago-
nally to your right. 你就可以看見國際學舍，在你的右側。

外國人： Fine. Thank you so much for your assistance.
好極了。謝謝你幫我那麼多的忙。

警　察： That's quite all right, sir. 不客氣，先生。

HINT BANK

・ ass istance〔əˈsɪstəns〕*n.* 幫助

＊注意" intead of to the right "不要漏掉" to "。

≡Grammar and Usage≡

1. 問路的說法

最常用" Excuse me, but ～."來開頭，也可以用" Pardon me, but ～."，" I beg your pardon, but ～."和"（I'm）Sorry to trouble you, but ～."

另外，一般習慣在" Excuse me "之後加上稱呼，男士用" sir "，女士用" ma'am "。如果是向警察問路，可以說" Excuse me, officer, but ～."

2. 被別人問路時

當別人問你" Could you direct me to ～?"或" Would you please tell me the way to ～? "時，如果你知道路時，就回答" Certainly."或" Of course."或" Surely."或" Sure."或" Okay." 等等。如果你不熟悉對方所問的路，可回答" I'm sorry, but I'm a stranger here myself."（對不起，在這裏我是個陌生人。）如果可能的話，可親切地再加上一點幫助的意見。如："Why don't you ask the policeman over there? "（你為何不問在那裏的警察？）或 " Please ask the man walking this way."（請你問走過來的這個人。）也可以說" I'll ask that policeman over there for you." （我幫你去問在那邊的警察。）

Fifth Week, Second Day

How to Give Directions for Boarding Conveyances

第五週，第二天　如何教別人搭車

BASIC DIALOGUES

1. **A**: Excuse me, but can you tell me *where to catch the bus for Yangmingshan*?

   對不起，不過可否請你告訴我，往陽明山的公車在哪裏搭乘？

   B: Certainly. The bus stop for Yangmingshan is just across the street. 當然，往陽明山的公車站牌，就在這條街的對面。

2. **A**: Pardon me, but can you tell me how I can go to Keelung? 對不起，不過可否請你告訴我，怎麼去基隆？

   B: Take the bus to Taipei Station and then transfer to the train which goes to Keelung.

   搭巴士到台北火車站，然後換搭開往基隆的火車。

3. **A**: *Which bus should I take to go to Kungkuan*?

   去公館要搭什麼公車？

B: Get on the No. 236 bus and get off at Kungkuan, which is the sixth stop from here.

搭二三六號公車，在公館下車，從這裡算起第六站。

4. A: *From which platform does the train for Kaohsiung leave*? 往高雄的火車，從哪一月台開出？

B: It leaves from platform 1. 從第一月台開出。

5. A: Does this train go to Taichung? 這班火車到台中嗎？

B: No, it doesn't. The train for Taichung leaves from platform 2. 不，沒有到，往台中的火車，從第二月台開出。

6. A: Can I get on this bus with this ticket?

我可以持這張票搭這班巴士嗎？

B: You need an express ticket as well as your regular train ticket. However, you can get an express ticket from a conductress in the bus.

除了普通車票，你還需要一張快車票。但是，你可以在車上向車掌買快車票。

7. A: Excuse me. Which way is the ticket window?

對不起，售票窗口怎麼走？

B: You'll find it down this way to the right.

你沿著這條路向右轉就會看到。

HINT BANK

- across〔ə'krɔs〕*prep.* 在…那邊　　　*transfer to ~* 換車
- platform〔'plæt,fɔrm〕*n.* 月台　　　express〔ɪk'sprɛs〕*n.* 特快巴士；快車
- *as well as* 除…外；和　　conductress〔kən'dʌktrɪs〕*n.* 車掌小姐
- *ticket window* 售票窗口

⬧ APPLIED CONVERSATION ⬧ 有關火車旅行的建議

Giving Advice for a Railroad Journey

外國人： Oh, David, I'm going to Kaohsiung next week, and when I get back, I'm taking a trip to Alishan.

喔，大衞，我下個星期要去高雄，回來時，要去阿里山旅行。

中國人： That's great, Helen！ *Have you gotten your train reservations for Kaohsiung*?

太棒了，海倫！去高雄的火車預售票你買了嗎？

外國人： Yes, my brother picked them up for me a few days ago.　I understand it's quite hard to get tickets.

買了，前幾天我弟弟把票拿給我了。我知道要買到票相當不容易。

中國人： Yes, the good trains are always crowded at this time of year.　You were lucky.　Which train are you taking?

是的，每年這個時候好的火車總是很擁擠，你很幸運，你搭哪一班火車？

HINT BANK ─────────────

・reservation〔͵rɛzə'veʃən〕*n.*（火車、旅館等的）預訂

＊ "Have you gotten your train reservations～?" " get "的過去分詞，美國人習慣用" gotten "，而英國人一般都用" got "。

外國人： I'm taking the Tzuchiang train that leaves Taipei
Station at 9. 我搭九點從台北車站開出的自強號。

中國人： It's one of Taiwan's best trains.
那是台灣最好的火車之一。

外國人： What time do you think I should be at the station?
你認為我什麼時候該到車站？

中國人： Since you have your reservations, ***there's no need to
be there early***... just be there before the train leaves.
既然你買了預售票，就不必太早去⋯，只要在火車要開之
前到就可以了。

外國人： Oh, yes, I wanted to ask you about Alishan. Is there
an express for Alishan, too?
喔，對了，我想問你有關阿里山的事。也有快車到阿里山嗎？

中國人： No. You must take a bus. 沒有，你最好搭巴士。

外國人： What is the best bus to take? 最好搭哪一班車？

中國人： I think there is a bus which leaves at 1:30 p.m.
and gets to Alishan about 4 o'clock in the evening.
我想有一班車，是下午一點半開出，大約傍晚四點抵達阿
里山。

外國人： ***That sounds good.*** Does it leave from Kaohsiung?
聽起來不錯。是從高雄開出的嗎？

中國人： No, that leaves from Chiayi. 不，是從嘉義開出的。

HINT BANK

＊“That sounds good.” 這裏的意思和 “That suits me fine.” 相似。

外國人： And how do I get to Chiayi？我要怎麼去嘉義？

中國人： Well, if you have lots of baggage, you'd better take a train. 呃，如果你有很多行李，最好是搭火車。

外國人： I'll just take an overnight bag. 我只帶一個小旅行袋。

中國人： Then you can go by bus. 那麼你可以搭巴士。

外國人： Good. I suppose the station name is Chiayi. 好。我想站名是嘉義吧。

中國人： That's right. 沒錯。

外國人： What's the fare？票價是多少？

中國人： The **bus fare I think is reasonable.** 我想車費不貴。

外國人： I suppose a taxi will cost three or four hundred dollars. 我想計程車需要三、四百元。

中國人： *I believe more than that.* 我認爲比那個還要多。

外國人： Well, I'll take the bus. 嗯，我要搭巴士。

HINT BANK ────────────

- baggage〔ˈbægɪdʒ〕*n.* 行李（ =〔英〕*luggage*）
- *overnight bag* 小旅行袋　　　fare〔fɛr〕*n.*（火車、公車、輪船等的）票價
- reasonable〔ˈriznəbḷ〕*adj.* 不貴的；合理的

═ Grammar and Usage ═

1. 表示「搭乘」的字

表示「搭乘」意思的英文有 "get on"，"take"，"ride" 等。"get on" 是「搭上」，著眼點在動作上。例：

· I *got* on a bus at Kungkuan.（我在公館搭巴士。）

"take" 有「乘～；利用（交通工具）」的意思。例：

· You had better *take* the train.（你最好搭火車。）

用 "take" 時，後面的受詞之前要加 "the"，如："take the bus"。如果用 "go by" 則後面的受詞不加冠詞，如："go by taxi"。

此外，"ride" 是指「乘騎」的動作，所以用在 "ride on a bicycle"（騎單車）或 "ride on a horse"（騎馬）等等的交通工具上。

2. 「月台」和「第～軌道」

我們中文說：「第～月台」，這是從英國式英語 "platform No. ～" 而來的。在美國則稱為 "Track No. ～"（第～軌道）。"track" 是指鐵軌，「單軌」是 "single track"，「雙軌」是 "double track"。

3. 火車站內，其他和乘車有關的字句用法

♤ 剪票口	*wicket, boarding gate*
♤ 賣票的窗口	*ticket window*
♤ 售票處	*ticket office*（美），*booking office*（英）
♤ 候車室	*waiting room, waiting lounge*
♤ 服務處	*information*（*desk*）
♤ 失物招領處	*lost and found*
♤ 站務員	*station employee*

Fifth Week, Third Day

On a Train

第五週,第三天 在火車上

BASIC DIALOGUES

1. A: Excuse me, but *is this seat taken*?
   對不起,請問這位子有沒有人坐?

   B: No, it isn't. Please sit down. 沒有。請坐。

2. A: How far are you going? 你要去什麼地方?

   B: I'm going as far as Kaohsiung. 我要去高雄。

3. A: Are you on a business trip? 你是因公旅行嗎?

   B: Well, *yes and no*. After doing some business in Kao-hsiung, I'm planning a visit to Chengching Lake for sightseeing. 哦,一半是,一半不是。在高雄談點生意後,我打算去澄清湖遊覽一番。

4. A: Have we passed Keelung yet? 我們經過基隆了嗎?

   B: I don't think so. 我想還沒有。

5. A: *How many stops* is Taichung from here?
   從這裏到台中有幾站?

B : It's three stops from here. This is an express train,
you know, so it doesn't stop at smaller stations.
從這裏算起有三站。這是快車，你知道，較小的站不停。

6. A : Do you know when we shall arrive in Kaohsiung?
你知道我們何時抵達高雄嗎？

B : According to the timetable, we should arrive at 3:30.
根據時刻表，我們三點半會抵達。

7. A : Do you think the train will arrive on time?
你認爲火車會準時到站嗎？

B : I'm sure it will. 我相信會。

8. A : Does this train have a dining car? 這列車有餐車嗎？

B : Yes. Shall we go to the diner?
有。我們去餐車用餐吧！

9. A : Can I see Mt. Yangmingshan from the window?
我從窗戶可以看到陽明山嗎？

B : I don't suppose you can. 我想你看不到。

10. A : Is this your first trip to Sun Moon Lake?
這是你第一次去日月潭嗎？

B : Yes. I've often visited Taichung, but I've never been
to Sun Moon Lake.是的。我時常去台中，但還沒去過日月潭。

HINT BANK───────────────

- *according to* 依照；據　　diner〔'daɪnɚ〕*n.* 餐車（= *dining car*）
- timetable〔'taɪm,tebḷ〕*n.* 時刻表

* "How far are you going?"用"How far～?"是明確地表示目的地的用法。

* "on time"是指「準時；按時」，而"in time"是指「及時；來得及」。

◀ APPLIED CONVERSATION ▶ 和同車的旅客聊天
Fellow Passengers on a Train

中國人： My name is Lin. It looks like we're going to be fellow passengers on this train.
我姓林。看來我們在這列車上是同座的旅客。

外國人： My name is Jackson. I'm very glad to meet you, Mr. Lin.
我是傑克生。很高興見到你，林先生。

中國人： It's a pleasure, Mr. Jackson. How far are you going?
我的榮幸，傑克生先生。你要到哪裡？

外國人： I'm going as far as Kaohsiung. And you?
我要去高雄。你呢？

中國人： I'm getting off at Taichung. Are you on a business trip, Mr. Jackson?
我將在台中下車。你是因公事而旅行嗎，傑克生先生？

外國人： Well, **half business, half pleasure**. I want to stop off on my way back and visit Tainan.
哦，一半是公事，一半是遊覽。我打算在回程的中途下車，去台南遊覽。

HINT BANK

* "fellow"是指「同在一處的；同伴的」，如："fellow passengers"（同車或同船者），"fellow countrymen"（同胞），"fellow students"（同學）。

中國人：How nice. Have you done much travelling in Taiwan?
　　　　眞好！你在台灣旅行過很多地方了嗎？

外國人：Well, ***I do quite a bit of*** travelling on business, but I
　　　　never seem to have the time to travel just for
　　　　enjoyment. 唔，我因為公事去過一些地方，但是似乎還沒
　　　　有時間純粹為遊玩而旅行。

中國人：Have you been in Taiwan a long time?
　　　　你在台灣很久了嗎？

外國人：Only for about six months. But I expect to stay here
　　　　for another two years or so.
　　　　大約只有六個月。但是我希望再住個二年左右。

中國人：Then you still have plenty of time to visit some of
　　　　the famous spots in Taiwan.
　　　　那麼，你還有許多時間可以參觀台灣的名勝。

外國人：Yes, I hope to see many of the beautiful places in
　　　　your country. I travel by air on most of my business
　　　　trips so I have very little opportunity of seeing the
　　　　lovely Taiwanese countryside.
　　　　是的，我希望看看貴國許多美麗的地方。我的商務旅行大
　　　　多搭乘飛機，因此沒什麼機會欣賞台灣鄉間的迷人景色。

中國人：Yes, but air travel is so quick and timesaving.
　　　　嗯，但是空中旅行既快又節省時間。

HINT BANK─────────────────

・timesaving〔'taɪm,sevɪŋ〕*adj.* 節省時間的

＊ " a bit " 是「一些，少許」，但是， " quite a bit of ～" 是指「相當多」的意思。

外國人： ***I don't know about that***. Sometimes it takes longer from the city to the airport than it does to go from Taipei to Kaohsiung by plane.

　　　　我不知道是否如此。有時候從城市到機場所花的時間，比從台北搭飛機到高雄所花的時間還久。

中國人： You're quite right. The traffic is awful！

　　　　你說的對。交通非常擁擠。

外國人： Have you had lunch？ If you haven't, shall we go to the diner ***for a bite to eat***？

　　　　你吃過午餐了嗎？如果還沒有，我們去餐車吃點東西好嗎？

中國人： That sounds like a good idea. 聽起來是個好主意。

外國人： Yes, but will you wait a minute？ I want to wash my hands. 是啊！但請你等一下好嗎？我想去洗手。

中國人： Certainly. ***Take your time***. I'll go to the diner first and reserve some seats for us.

　　　　當然好。不急，慢慢來。我先去餐車預訂座位。

外國人： Good. ***I'll join you in a few minutes***.

　　　　好。我等會兒就去找你。

HINT BANK―――――――――――――――

・ reserve〔rɪˈzɜv〕*v.* 預訂（座位、門票等）

＊ "wash my hands" 是「洗手」的意思，也可以用來指「上廁所」的意思。

Grammar and Usage

在公車或火車上，常有機會和外國人交談，有幾個用法必須注意：

1. 有關座位的問題

當有空位時，可以用下列句子來詢問別人：

- Is this seat *taken*?（有人坐這位子嗎？）
- Is this seat *occupied*?（這位子是空的嗎？）
- Can I *have* this seat?（我可以坐這位子嗎？）
- *Is it all right for me* to take this seat?
  （我可以坐這位子嗎？）

如果別人用"Is this seat taken?"來問你，位子若沒人坐，就回答"No, it isn't."。若有人要坐，就回答"I'm afraid it is (taken)."

2. 「有幾站？」的用法

在車上，常會有人問到：「到～之前還有幾站？」，如：

- How many stops is Kaohsiung from here?
  （從這裏到高雄有幾站？）

因為是指「停車的地方」，所以，是用"stop"而不用"station"。

3. 「這裏是哪裏？」的用法

中國人常誤用"Where is here?"來表示「這裏是哪裏？」，正確的用法是"*Where are we*?"（我們在哪裏？）這是很簡單的日常生活會話，但是，英文和中文的表達方式不同，所以，必須特別注意。

Fifth Week, Fourth Day

On the Telephone

第五週，第四天　在電話中

) BASIC DIALOGUES (

1. A : Hello. Is this the Wang residence ?
　　　嗨，這是王公館嗎？

　B : Yes, it is. 是的。

　A : May I speak to Mr. Wang, please ?
　　　我可以請王生先聽電話嗎？

2. A : Hello. This is John speaking. Is this Mr. Carter ?
　　　嗨，我是約翰，你是卡特先生嗎？

　B : Yes, speaking. 是的，我就是，請講。

3. A : This is Helen speaking. Is Mary at home ?
　　　我是海倫，瑪莉在家嗎？

　B : *I beg your pardon ? Could you speak a little louder ?*
　　　對不起，可否請你說大聲一點？

　A : Certainly. Is Mary at home ? Can you hear me now ?
　　　好的，瑪莉在家嗎？你現在可以聽見我在說什麼嗎？

B : Yes. Please hold the line a moment.

　　是的，請稍候。

4. A : Hello. *I'd like to speak to* Mr. Baker.

　　　嗨，請貝克爾先生聽電話。

B : One moment, please... I'm sorry he is out now. Will
you leave a message ?

　　請稍待…很抱歉他現在出去了。請你留話好嗎？

A : Yes. Could you ask him to call me back ?

　　你可否請他回電話給我？

B : Yes. May I ask your name ?

　　是的，請教尊姓大名？

A : Carter, George Carter.

　　卡特，喬治‧卡特。

5. A : *Can I reach him by telephone* ?

　　　我可以用電話聯絡到他嗎？

B : Yes, you can. His telephone number is 341-2785.

　　是的，他的電話號碼是三四一‧二七八五。

HINT BANK────────────

* " Is this the Wang residence?"這是電話用語，雖然是指對方，也用 " this "
　來稱呼。
* 在電話中，表示「我是～」的用語是 "This is～speaking." 也可以省略
　" speaking " 直接用 " This is ～." 表示。而 "Yes, speaking." 是 " Yes,
　this is～speaking." 的省略，是「我就是」的意思。
* " One moment, please." 是 " Please wait one moment." 的省略。也可
　以說成 " Just a moment, please."。

6. A : This is the Far East Trading Company.

這是遠東貿易公司。

   B : Extension 231, please.

請接內線二三一。

7. A : Is this the home of Mrs. Palmer ?

這是帕莫太太的家嗎？

   B : I'm sorry it isn't. I think you have the wrong number. This is 961-7967.

很抱歉，這不是。我想你打錯電話號碼了。這是九六一‧七九六七。

8. A : Hello. Is Tom there ?

喂，請問湯姆在嗎？

   B : Yes. May I ask who's calling, please ?

他在。請問是誰找他？

   A : Yes, this is Mike.

我是麥克。

HINT BANK ─────────────────────

· extension〔ɪk'stɛnʃən〕 *n.*（電話）內線

◄ APPLIED CONVERSATION ► 在朋友的辦公室打電話
Making a Call from a Friend's Office

中 國 人： May I use your telephone,
George ?

喬治，我可以借用一下你的
電話嗎？

喬　治： Certainly, John. *Just dial zero first* and then the number you want.

當然，約翰。只要先撥個零，然後再撥你要的號碼。

中 國 人： Thanks. 謝謝。

(Sound of telephone dialing / 撥電話的聲音)------------

總　機： Pacific Trading Company. May I help you ?

太平洋貿易公司，有什麼可以效勞的？

中 國 人： This is Mr. Wang speaking. Could you connect me with Mr. Brown ?

我姓王，可否請你幫我接布朗先生？

總　機： Certainly, sir. Will you hold the line a moment ?

好的，先生，請稍待。

中 國 人： Yes, of course. 是的，當然。

總　機： Mr. Brown is on the line, sir. 布朗先生接電話了，先生。

HINT BANK ─────────────────────

· connect〔kə'nɛkt〕v. 接通

＊ "Just dial zero first." 在命令句的句首加"just"，語氣較爲溫和。

中 國 人：Hello. Mr. Brown？嗨，布朗先生嗎？

布朗先生：Yes. Mr. Wang？ I was waiting for your call all
morning.

　　　　是的，王先生嗎？我整個早上都在等你的電話。

中 國 人：I'm so sorry, Mr. Brown. I was out at one of our
construction sites and couldn't call you.

　　　　非常抱歉，布朗先生。我在外頭我們公司的某個建築工地，
沒辦法打電話給你。

布朗先生：Now, let me see… Could you come to my office at
2 o'clock tomorrow afternoon？ *I'd like to discuss a
few things with you then*.

　　　　嗯，讓我想一想，可否請你明天下午兩點到我的辦公室？
到時，我想跟你討論一些事情。

中 國 人：Of course. Mr. Brown. I'll be going out to another
construction site tomorrow morning, so I won't be
in my office until noon. If by any chance you wish
to get in touch with me, could you please leave a
message with my secretary？

　　　　當然，布朗先生。明天早上我要出去到另外一個建築工地，
所以中午以前我不會在辦公室。如果萬一你想跟我聯絡的
話，可否請你留話給我的祕書？

布朗先生：Yes, I'll do that. At any rate I'll see you here at
2 o'clock tomorrow.

　　　　好的，我會的。無論如何，明天兩點在這兒見。

HINT BANK──────────────

- *construction sites* 建築工地　　*by any chance* 萬一
- *leave a message with* 留話給～　　*at any rate* 無論如何（＝*in any case*）

中 國 人： ***I'll be there without fail***. Goodbye, Mr. Brown.
　　　　　　我一定會到。再見，布朗先生。

布朗先生： Goodbye, Mr. Wang. 再見，王先生。

（ Sound of receiver being replaced ╱話筒放回去的聲音）----------

喬　　治： All through? 通話完畢了嗎？

中 國 人： Yes, thanks. 是的，謝謝。

喬　　治： Say, how about coming home with me for dinner?
　　　　　　嘿，跟我回家一起吃晚飯如何？

中 國 人： But it would be so much trouble for Helen.
　　　　　　不過，這樣給海倫太多麻煩了。

喬　　治： Oh, my wife wouldn't mind. I'll call her and tell
　　　　　　her you're coming.
　　　　　　喔，我太太不會在意的。我會打電話給她，告訴她，你來
　　　　　　了。

中 國 人： Well, if you insist. 嗯，如果你堅持的話。

HINT BANK————————————

・ ***without fail*** 無誤；必定　　　through〔θru〕 *adv.* （通話）結束（＝*finished*）

＊ “ It would be so much trouble for Helen. ”用“ would ”是表示用站在「如
　果我去的話」的立場上來說。

◢ Fifth Week, Fifth Day ◣

In a Store

第五週，第五天 在商店中

▶ BASIC DIALOGUES ◀

1. A : Good afternoon. May I help you?

午安。我能爲你效勞嗎？

B : I'd like to see some neckties. 我想要看些領帶。

2. A : What can I do for you, sir? 我能爲您做什麼呢，先生？

B : *Where can I find* Chinese china?

我在哪裏可以找到中國瓷器？

A : They're on the fifth floor, sir. 它們在五樓，先生。

3. A : What's the price of this stereo set? 這組音響要多少錢？

B : It's 18,900 dollars. 要一萬八千九百元。

A : My, that's quite expensive. Is that the only kind you have? 天啊！相當貴哪！那是你們唯一有的類型嗎？

B : No, ma'am. This one over here is cheaper. It's 9,500 dollars. 不，女士，在這邊的這台就比較便宜了，它要九千五百元。

4. A： Could you show me that suitcase, please？

　　　　請問你能給我看看那個手提箱嗎？

　 B： Certainly, ma'am. This one？ 當然，女士，是這一個嗎？

　 A： No, the one next to it. 不，旁邊的那一個。

　 B： Here you are. 這個便是。

5. A： Do you sell this television set on the installment plan？

　　　　你們是以分期付款的方式，出售這台電視機嗎？

　 B： Yes. You can pay in 10 monthly installments.

　　　　是的，你可以用十個月來分期付款。

6. A： Can you have it delivered, please？ 能請你把它送來嗎？

　 B： Certainly, ma'am. Where would you like it to be delivered？

　　　　當然，女士，你想把它送到哪裏呢？

　 A： This is my address. When can I expect to have it？

　　　　這是我的地址。我什麼時候可收到呢？

　 B： We can have it delivered to you by Saturday without fail.

　　　　我們在星期六以前，一定把它送達你那裏。

7. A： How much is it？ 這個多少錢？

　 B： Fifty-five hundred, ma'am. 五千五百元，女士。

　 A： Here's the money. 錢在這裏。

　 B： Six thousand dollars... Please wait a minute... This is
　　　　the change...five hundred dollars. Thank you very much.

　　　　六千元…請等一下…這是找錢…五百元，非常謝謝你。

HINT BANK——————————

• deliver〔dɪ'lɪvɚ〕 *v.* 遞送；交付

＊ 商店的店員常用 " May I help you?"或"What can I do for you?"來招呼客人。

＊ " Fifty-five hundred" 可以唸成 "Five thousand, five hundred dollars."

◄ APPLIED CONVERSATION ► 在服飾店
At a Clothing Store

中國人： Good afternoon. *Is there*
something I can do for you?
午安。我能為你做什麼嗎？

外國人： Yes, I'd like to see some shirts.
是的，我想看些襯衫。

中國人： Yes, sir. This way, please.
好的，先生。請往這兒走。

外國人： Could you show me something in stripes?
能給我看些有條紋的嗎？

中國人： These are quite nice, sir. May I ask what size you wear?
這些相當好，先生。請問你穿多大的尺寸？

外國人： I wear a 15-inch neck and a 32-inch sleeve.
我穿領子十五吋和袖子三十二吋的。

中國人： This is your size, sir. 這是你的尺寸，先生。

外國人： How much is this? 這要多少錢？

中國人： These are 400 dollars. 這些要四百元。

外國人： All right, I'll take two of them. 好的，我要二件。

中國人： Would you like both in blue stripes?
你要二件都是藍色條紋的嗎？

HINT BANK

• stripe〔straɪp〕*n.* 條紋

外國人：Let me see... I think you'd better give me *one with* blue stripes *and the other with* brown stripes.

讓我想想…。我想最好給我一件藍色條紋，另一件咖啡色條紋的。

中國人：Yes, sir. That will be just 800 dollars.

好的，先生。正好八百元。

外國人：Could you have them delivered？你能把它們送來嗎？

中國人：Of course, sir. *May I have your address, please*?

當然，先生，請告訴我你的住址。

外國人：No. 5, 4th Floor, Alley 6, Lane 96, Ho-ping E. Road, Section 2.

和平東路二段96巷6弄5號4樓。

中國人：And the name, sir？姓名呢？先生。

外國人：Thomas Jackson. *When can I expect delivery*?

湯瑪斯・傑克生。我能在何時收到呢？

中國人：They'll go out in the first delivery tomorrow morning. You should receive them before noon.

他們將在明早第一批發送，你應可在中午以前收到。

外國人：Thank you very much.

非常謝謝你。

HINT BANK

* 詢問別人住址的句型，通常用："May I have your address, please？"
* "You should receive them before noon." 用 "should" 是表示「當然應該」的意思。

中國人：Thank you, sir. *Please come again.*

謝謝，先生。請下次再度光臨。

外國人：Oh, yes, do you have neckties here？

噢，好的，這裏有賣領帶嗎？

中國人：Yes, sir. The necktie counter is at the end of this corridor.

有的，先生。賣領帶的專櫃在這條走道的盡頭。

外國人：I see. And what about sporting goods？

我知道了。那麼運動用品呢？

中國人：The sporting goods department is on the fifth floor. You can take the escalator to your right, or the elevator to your left.

運動用品部在五樓，你可以搭在你右邊的自動梯，或是你左邊的電梯。

外國人：Thank you so much. 非常謝謝你。

中國人：Not at all, sir. 不用客氣，先生。

HINT BANK

• goods〔gʊdz〕*n. pl.* 貨物　　escalator〔'ɛskə,letə〕*n.* 自動梯
• elevator〔'ɛlə,vetə〕*n.* 電梯

Grammar and Usage

在美國，一般稱商店為"*store*"，而在英國則稱為"*shop*"。在商店中，有一些基本的用法，現說明如下：

1.「歡迎」

常有人以為"Welcome."是用來表示「歡迎」的意思。但是，一般的店員，並不使用這種說法。通常用"Good morning."或"Good afternoon."或"Good evening."或"How do you do?"來打招呼而已。有時也用"May I help you?"（我能為你效勞嗎？）或"What can I do for you?"（我可以為你做什麼嗎？）來招呼客人。

2.「請拿～給我看」

這個說法通常用"I'd like to see ～."（我想看～。）或用"Could you show me ～?"（你能拿～給我看嗎？）其他還可以用下列的方式來表示。

· Where can I find ～?（我在哪裏可以找到～？）
· Where's the ～ department?（～部在哪裏？）
· May I take a look at ～ on the shelf there?
（我可以看擺在那邊架上的～嗎？）

3. 關於價格

問「多少錢？」，通常用"How much is it?"或"How much are they?"也有人用"What's the price（of ～）?"

「貴」是用"expensive"，「便宜」是用"inexpensive"或"cheap"，「減價」是用"beat down the price"，「打折」是用"make a discount"。

Fifth Week, Sixth Day

An Interview

第五週，第六天　會面

▶ BASIC DIALOGUES ◀

1. **A** : *I'd like to make an appointment with* Mr. Baxter. Will you please ask him when he'll be free to see me?

   我想和巴克斯特先生訂個約會，能請你問他何時有空可以見我嗎？

   B : Certainly sir. Wait a moment, please... Sorry to have kept you waiting. He says he'd be glad to see you between 2 and 3 this afternoon, if it would be all right with you.

   當然，先生，請等一下⋯。很抱歉讓你久等，他說如果你可以的話，他很樂意在今天下午二點到三點之間見你。

2. **A** : Could you arrange an interview with the president for me? 能請你幫我安排一個與校長見面的時間嗎？

   B : *What time would be most convenient for you?*

   什麼時間對你最方便？

A : Tomorrow afternoon is most convenient, but any time would be all right for me.

明天下午最方便，但對我來說什麼時間都行。

3. A : Would it be possible to have an interview with Mr. Lee now? 現在可以和李先生見面嗎？

B : Please wait a moment. I'll ask him if he is free for an interview. 請等一下，我去問他是否有會面的時間。

4. A : *I don't have an appointment*, but could I see Mr. Wang just a few minutes?

我沒有事先約好，不過我能不能見王先生，幾分鐘就好了？

B : I'm very sorry, but he meets people only by appointment.

我非常抱歉，但是他只和有約的人見面。

5. A : My name is Jack Wilson. I'd like to see Mr. Saunders.

我叫傑克·威爾遜，我想見梭德先生。

B : Do you have an appointment? 你事先有約好嗎？

A : Yes, I have an appointment for 3 o'clock.

是的，我有約在三點鐘。

B : Please wait a moment.... I'm sorry to have kept you waiting. Mr. Saunders will be here in a moment.

請等一下，…抱歉讓你久等，梭德先生馬上就來。

HINT BANK─────────────────

· *make an appointment with ~* 和~有約　　*be free~* 有空

· *arrange an interview with ~* 安排和~見面

* "have an appointment for 3 o'clock" 要特別注意介系詞是用 "for"。

◀ APPLIED CONVERSATION ▶ 請求會面

Seeking an Interview

祕　書：Good afternoon, sir. Did you wish to see Mr. Baxter?
午安，先生。你想見巴克斯特先生嗎？

中國人：Yes, *I wonder if I could see him for a few minutes.*
是的，我不知是否可以見他幾分鐘。

祕　書：Will you have a seat, please? I'll see if Mr. Baxter is free.
請坐。我看看巴克斯特先生是不是有空。

中國人：Thank you very much. 非常謝謝。

（Speaking into intercom／用對講機講話）-------------

祕　書：Mr. Baxter, there is a gentleman in my office to see you. 巴克斯特先生，在我辦公室這兒有位先生要見你。

外國人：Who is it, Susan? 蘇珊，是誰？

祕　書：*May I ask who is calling?* 請問是哪一位？

HINT BANK────────────────────────

・intercom〔'ɪntə,kɑm〕*n*. 對講機

＊*t* "Who is it?" 因為還沒看到對方，所以用 "it"，而不用 "he"。

＊ "May I ask who is calling?" 這是用在傳達問訪客的姓名時，如果是自己接見訪客，就用 "May I ask your name?" 來問對方。

中國人：Lee...John Lee. 李⋯李約翰。

祕　書：Mr. John Lee. 是李約翰先生。

外國人：He doesn't have an appointment, does he?
　　　　他沒有事先約定，不是嗎？

祕　書：No, sir, he doesn't. 沒有，先生，他沒有。

外國人：***Will you ask him to wait***? I'm having a conference
　　　　now, but I should be through in about 20 minutes.
　　　　請你讓他等一下好嗎？我正在開會，但是我將在約二十分鐘
　　　　內結束。

祕　書：Yes, sir. 好的，先生。

祕　書：Mr. Lee, Mr. Baxter is in conference. ***He'll be
　　　　finished in about*** 20 ***minutes***. Could you wait?
　　　　李先生，巴克斯特先生正在開會，他將在二十分鐘內結束。
　　　　你能等一下嗎？

中國人：Let me see... don't believe I can. I'll just leave my
　　　　card. I'll telephone him tomorrow and ask for an ap-
　　　　pointment.
　　　　讓我考慮一下⋯我想不能，我暫時留下我的名片，在明天打
　　　　電話給他，並約個時間見面。

祕　書：I'm so sorry, Mr. Lee. I think Mr. Baxter will be
　　　　free tomorrow afternoon. If you could call him in the
　　　　morning, I'm sure he will see you in the afternoon.
　　　　抱歉，李先生，我想巴克斯特先生明天下午有空，如果你
　　　　能在上午打電話給他，他將在下午見你。

中國人：Thank you so much. 多謝了。

秘 書： *Would you care to leave a message*？
　　　　你想留下些話嗎？

中國人： Will you please tell him that I can give him a ring
　　　　before 9 o'clock tomorrow morning？
　　　　能請你轉告他，我在明早九點以前會打電話給他嗎？

秘 書： Could you make that sometime between 9:30 and 10
　　　　o'clock？ Mr. Baxter usually arrives at the office
　　　　shortly after 9 o'clock.
　　　　你能在九點半到十點之間打電話嗎？巴克斯特先生通常在
　　　　九點多到辦公室。

中國人： Certainly. 當然可以。

秘 書： I'm sorry you can't wait to see Mr. Baxter.
　　　　我很遺憾你不能等著見巴克斯特先生。

中國人： I am too, but I have another appointment. Thank you
　　　　again.
　　　　我也一樣，但我另有約會。再次謝謝你。

秘 書： Don't mention it. Goodbye. 別客氣，再見。

HINT BANK───────────

• *give one a ring* 打電話給…　　shortly〔ˊʃɔrtlɪ〕*adv.* 不久；即刻

* " Would you care to leave a message？" 句中用 " care to＋V " 表示「想
　做～」。

Grammar and Usage

1. 會面的約定

英美人要與人見面，或拜訪對方時，大都會事先以電話或書信和對方先約好。尤其是有關工作的會面，一定要有 " appointment "（會面的約定）。

在與人作會面的約定，可以直接用電話和對方本人相約，或透過祕書來連絡。若直接和對方本人相約時，可以說：

- Could I see you sometime this afternoon?
  （今天下午我可以見你嗎？）

如果是透過祕書連絡時，可以說：

- I'd like to make an appointment with ～.
  （我想和～約個會面時間。）
- Could you arrange an interview with ～ for me?
  （你能為我安排和～見面嗎？）

2. 表示「方便」或「不方便」的用語

「（沒）有時間」是用 " have (no) time to ～ " 或 " be (not) free to ～ " 來表示。「（不）方便」用 " be (not) convenient " 在 " convenient " 之後的介系詞用 " for " 或 " to "。

- Tomorrow could be *convenient* for me.
  （明天對我很適合〔方便〕。）

也可以用動詞 " suit " 來表示：

- Does Sunday *suit* you?（禮拜天你方便嗎？）

與熟識的英美朋友聊天

6th Week   Conversations with American and English Friends

Sixth Week, First Day

On the Weather

第六週，第一天　談天氣

> **BASIC DIALOGUES**

1. A : *It's a fine day, isn't it* ? 今天天氣很好，不是嗎？

　B : Yes, isn't it ? I hope this fine weather will last for a few more days.

　　是的，可不是？我希望這種好天氣多持續幾天。

2. A : Do you think it'll be fine tomorrow?

　　你想明天天氣會晴朗嗎？

　B : I'm sure it will. But it's so cold I suppose it'll be freezing tonight.

　　我確信會的。不過，太冷了，我想今晚天氣會酷寒。

3. A : I'm going to Lishan this weekend. 這個週末我要去梨山。

　B : That's wonderful. But take care, for it may rain in the mountains. 太棒了。不過當心，山區可能會下雨。

4. A : We had a terrible typhoon last night, didn't we?

　　我們昨晚渡過了一個可怕的颱風，不是嗎？

B： We surely did. I couldn't sleep a wink all night.
的確是，整晚我都不能闔眼。

5. A： What's the weather forecast for today？
今天的天氣預報怎麼說？

B： It says cloudy in the morning, but it'll clear up early in the afternoon.
天氣預報說晨間多雲，不過下午很早就會放晴。

6. A： *How's the weather today*？ 今天天氣如何？

B： It looks like rain. You'd better take your umbrella with you. 看起來像是要下雨，你最好帶傘。

7. A： I told her I would pay a visit to her this afternoon if it wasn't raining.
我告訴過她，如果沒下雨的話，今天下午我會去拜訪她。

B： Lots of luck. *It's raining cats and dogs.*
真幸運，下傾盆大雨。

8. A： It's terribly hot, isn't it？ I wonder what the thermometer reads. 熱死了，不是嗎？我想知道現在氣溫幾度。

B： It says 95 degrees！ I can't stand this heat.
九十五度！我受不了這種熱度。

HINT BANK ─────────────

· freeze〔friz〕*v.* 凍冷；酷寒　　*take care* 當心；注意
· *sleep a wink* 闔眼（＝ *get a wink of sleep*）　　*weather forecast* 天氣預報
· *clear up* （天氣）放晴　　*rain cats and dogs* 傾盆大雨
· thermometer〔θə'mɑmətə〕*n.* 溫度計

＊"Yes，isn't it？"這是附和的用法，語尾的音調要下降。

◀APPLIED CONVERSATION▶ 談天氣

Tallking about the Weather

中國人： Hi Bill. ***All ready for
the trip to Hohuanshan
next week？***
嗨，比爾，下週到合歡山
之行準備好了嗎？

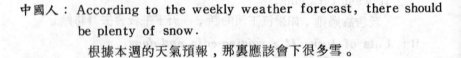

外國人： Good morning, James. I
still must get a few things
to take on the trip.
早安，詹姆斯。我還必須買一些旅行要帶的東西。

中國人： According to the weekly weather forecast, there should
be plenty of snow.
根據本週的天氣預報，那裏應該會下很多雪。

外國人： Good. It's been so warm here in Taipei that I wondered whether there would be enough snow for skiing.
很好，台北這裏這麼熱，我眞懷疑那裏是不是有足夠的雪可
滑雪。

中國人： ***The weatherman says we'll have a cold spell before the
end of this week.***
天氣預報的人說，在這個週末之前，會有一陣子冷天氣。

HINT BANK───────────────────

• weekly〔'wiklı〕*adj*. 每週的　weatherman〔'wɛðɚ,mæn〕*n*. 擔任天氣預報的人
• spell〔spɛl〕*n*. 一段時間

* " All ready for～？"前面省略了" Are you"。

外國人：Well, I hope so. There's not much sense going skiing some place where there's no snow.

嗯，我希望如此。到某個不下雪的地方滑雪,沒有多大意思。

中國人：I wouldn't worry about that. 我就不擔心這點了。

外國人：Whew, it certainly is an awful day today.

咻，今天眞是可怕的一天。

中國人：*It certainly is*！It started raining about five o'clock this morning, didn't it？

的確是！從今天早上五點左右就開始下雨，不是嗎？

外國人：Well, it was only a drizzle when I got up at 7 o'clock, but it's a regular rainstorm now.

嗯，七點起床時，只下毛毛雨，不過，現在下起標準的暴風雨。

中國人：Hasn't the weather been awfully peculiar this year？

今年天氣不是太特殊了嗎？

外國人：I should say so. The summer was so hot and sultry.

的確是如此，以往的夏天是又熱又悶。

中國人：Remember that terrible typhoon？

記得那個可怕的颱風嗎？

HINT BANK

- awful〔'ɔfʊl〕*adj.*（暴風雨等）可怕的；驚人的
- drizzle〔'drɪzl̩〕*v.* 下毛毛雨；下細雨的
- rainstorm〔'ren,stɔrm〕*n.* 暴風雨
- peculiar〔pɪ'kjuljɚ〕*adj.* 特殊的；下細雨（ = *special* ）
- sultry〔'sʌltrɪ〕*adj.* 悶熱的；溽暑的　　typhoon〔taɪ'fun〕*n.* 颱風

外國人 : I certainly do. That was quite a storm. We're lucky
that the center of the storm missed us.
當然記得,好大的暴風雨。我們運氣好,沒有在暴風雨的中心 。

中國人 : We certainly are. I understand they still haven't been
able to rebuild many of the houses destroyed by the
typhoon.
的確是 ,我知道有許多被颱風毀壞的房子 ,他們還無法重建。

外國人 : *It's certainly a shame*. 真可憐 。

中國人 : Do you think this rain will let up today ?
你想這雨今天會停息嗎 ?

外國人 : It's raining pretty hard, but it might clear up this
afternoon. If it does, I want to go out and do some
shopping. 雨下得好大 ,不過 ,可能今天下午會放晴 。如果放
晴的話 ,我想出去買點東西 。

中國人 : Is there anything in particular you want to buy ?
還有任何你特別想要買的東西嗎 ?

外國人 : Well, I thought I'd look at some ski boots. Mine are
quite old and I really need a new pair.
嗯,我想看看滑雪靴。我的相當舊,而且我真的需要一雙新的。

中國人 : *Mind if I come along* ? I want to look at some of the
new imported skis.
你不介意我一道去吧?我想看看新的進口靴 。

外國人 : Not at all. 一點也不 。

HINT BANK━━━━━━━━━━━━━━━━━━━━

· rebuild〔ri'bɪld〕v · 重建 ;改建　　*let up* (暴風雨等)停息

═ Grammar and Usage ═

1. 談天氣打招呼

外國人，尤其是英美人，常以天氣作爲話題。用天氣來當作話題，不僅可以避免爭論，還可以代替寒喧，而以輕鬆的語氣展開談話的內容。如：

- It's a fine day, isn't it? — Yes, isn't it?
  （天氣很好，不是嗎？）　　（是的，可不是嗎？）
- It's terribly hot, isn't it? — It certainly is.
  （天氣好熱，不是嗎？）　　（的確如此。）

從以上的例子，可以知道以天氣的話題作爲寒喧，在回答時，通常都是用 "*Yes, isn't it?*" 或 "*It certainly is.*" 等附和的句子。

2. 天氣的問法

以下列舉幾個有關天氣的問法：

- What's the weather like today?（今天天氣如何？）
- What's the weather forecast for today?
  （今天的氣象報告怎麼樣〔報告〕？）
- What does the paper say about tomorrow's weather?
  （關於明天的天氣，報紙上怎麼說？）
- What does the radio forecast say?
  （收音機的天氣預報怎麼說？）

3. 表示天氣的主詞用 *It*

「晴天」用 " be fine "，「陰天」用 " be cloudy "，「下雨」用 " rain "，「下雪」用 " snow "，「暖和」用 " be warm "，「寒冷」用 " be cold " 等表示方法，其主詞通常用 " it "，很少用 " the weather "。

Sixth Week, Second Day

Visiting

第六週，第二天　拜　訪

BASIC DIALOGUES

1. A : Will it be all right to visit you this evening ?
   今天晚上去看你好嗎 ?

   B : I'm very sorry, but I have an appointment this evening.
   How about tomorrow evening ?
   很抱歉，我今晚有個約會。明晚如何 ?

2. A : Do you mind if we call on you this evening ?
   你介不介意我們今晚去拜訪你 ?

   B : Of course not. We'd be happy if you could come. What
   time will you be able to come ?
   當然不，如果你能來的話，我們會很高興。你什麼時候能來 ?

   A : How about seven ? 七點如何 ?

   B : Fine. We'll be expecting you. 很好。我們恭候大駕。

3. A : Is this Mr. Smith's residence ? 這是史密斯先生公館嗎 ?

   B : Yes, it is. 是的。

A : My name is David. Is Mr. Smith at home ?
　　我叫大衞，史密斯先生在家嗎？

B : Yes, he is in. Please wait a moment.
　　是的，他在。請等一會兒。

4. **A :** *How nice of you to come* ! 你來眞好！

　　B : It's been a long time, hasn't it ? *How have you been*?
　　　　好久（不見）了，不是嗎？近來好嗎？

　　A : Just fine, thanks. And you ? 很好，謝謝。你呢？

　　B : I've never been better, thanks.
　　　　我從來沒有比現在更好過（現在再好也不過了）。謝謝。

5. **A :** Please take a seat and *make yourself comfortable*.
　　　　請坐，不要拘束。

　　B : Thank you. 謝謝。

6. **A :** It's four o'clock already. I hate to leave, but I think
　　　　I must. 已經四點了。眞不想走，但是，我還是得走。

　　B : Can't you stay a little longer ? 你不能再多待一會兒嗎？

　　A : I'm very sorry, but I can't. 很抱歉，但是我不能。

7. **B :** I had a wonderful evening. 我渡過了一個美好的夜晚。

　　A : I did, too. Come and visit us again, won't you ?
　　　　我也是，再來看我們，好嗎？

　　B : Thank you, I will. 謝謝你，我會的。

HINT BANK────────────────────

・ *call on* 拜訪（ = *visit*)　　hate〔het〕*v.* 〔口〕極討厭；極不願（=*regret*)

* " make yourself comfortable " 是請別人「不要太拘束、客氣」。可以用" at
home " 來替換 " comfortable " 。

⧓ APPLIED CONVERSATION ⧓　拜訪朋友

Paying a Visit to a Friend's House

中國人：Good evening, Mr. Brown.
晚安，布朗先生。

布　朗：Good evening, David. Good
evening, Mrs. Lai. *It was
so good of you both to
come*. 晚安，大衞。晚安，賴太
太，你們兩個人都來眞好。

中國人：*It was nice of you to invite us*. 你邀我們來，眞好。

布　朗：Not at all. Do come in. 一點也不（不要謝）。請進。

（Sound of door closing／關門的聲音 ）----------

布　朗：Here, let me take your things. Oh, Alice, Mr. and
Mrs. Lai are here. 嘿，我幫你拿東西。喔，愛麗絲，賴
先生和賴太太在這裏。

愛麗絲：Why, good evening. How nice of you to come！
哎呀，晚安。你們來眞好！

布　朗：Mr. and Mrs. Johnson are here. I believe you met
Mr. Johnson in my office the other day.
詹森先生和詹森太太在這裏。我想你前幾天在我的辦公室
見過詹森先生。

HINT BANK

* " Do come in." 句中用 " Do " 是表示強調語氣。

中 國 人： Yes, of course. How do you do, Mr. Johnson ? It's nice to meet you again.

是的，當然。詹森先生，你好嗎？再度見到你眞好。

詹　　森： How do you do, Mr. Lai ? This is Mrs. Johnson.... Mr. and Mrs. Lai.

賴先生，你好嗎？這是詹森太太…賴先生及賴太太。

詹森太太： I'm very happy to meet you both.

非常高興見到你們兩位。

布　　朗： Now, David, ***can I get you a drink*** ? What will you have? 那麼，大衞，我拿杯飲料給你好嗎？你要喝什麼？

中 國 人： A Scotch and soda, please.

冰蘇格蘭威士忌蘇打，麻煩你。

布　　朗： What about you, Alice ? 愛麗絲，你呢？

愛 麗 絲： Cola is fine, thank you. 可樂就好了，謝謝你。

布　　朗： All right, I'll bring you a Cola. How about you, Bob ? Can I bring you another drink ?

好的，我拿杯可樂給你。鮑伯，你呢？我再拿杯飲料給你好嗎？

詹　　森： No thanks, Fred. As a matter of fact I must be leaving. ***I have some work I have to catch up on.***

不，謝謝，弗瑞德。事實上，我必須走了。我有些工作必須要完成。

HINT BANK───────────────

・ ***catch up*** 完成；不落後

＊ " Scotch and soda "是指「冰蘇格蘭威士忌蘇打」，是屬於 " highball "（攙汽水酒），威士忌加汽水的一種。

布　朗：Must you leave so early? We would really like you
　　　　to stay a while longer.
　　　　你必須這麼早離開嗎？我們眞的很希望你多留一會兒？

詹　森：I'm sorry, but I'm afraid that it can't wait.
　　　　抱歉，恐怕這不能等。

布　朗：Well, we'll have to set another date so we can all
　　　　have dinner together.
　　　　嗯，我們必須另訂日期，這樣我們才能都在一起吃飯。

詹　森：That would be fine. It's a pleasure to have met you
　　　　again, Mr. Lai, and Mrs. Lai too. I hope we meet
　　　　again soon.
　　　　這樣很好。賴先生，賴太太再度見到你們眞是榮幸，希望
　　　　我們很快就會再度見面。

中 國 人：Yes, indeed. 是的，的確是。

═ Grammar and Usage ═

1. 表示「拜訪」的用法

在英文中，含有「拜訪」意思的用法："*visit*"，"*pay a visit to ～*"，"*call on*"，"*call at*"，"*drop in on*"…等等。通常"visit"所停留的時間較長，而"drop in on"是指「順道來訪」之意。但是雖然如此，在使用上，沒有嚴格的劃分。不過，要注意的是"call on"的受詞是「人」，而"call at"的受詞是「地方」。例：

- May I *call on* you tomorrow？"（明天我可以去拜訪你嗎？）
- I *called at* his home yesterday.（昨天我去拜訪他家。）

"drop in on"的受詞也是「人」，如果沒有受詞，就只用"drop in"。例：

- Please *drop in* any time.（請隨時來訪。）

2. 在「告辭」時的用語

中國人在離開別人家時，通常會很客氣地說聲：「打擾了。」但是，如果對英美人說"I'm very sorry to have interrupted you."對方可能會懷疑，你是不是真的認為打擾了而道歉。所以，這句話不適合在告辭使用。

他們在告辭時，通常會對主人說"*I had a wonderful time.*"（我渡過一段美好的時光。）此時，主人會客氣地說"*I'm glad you could come.*"（很高興你能來。）或"*I enjoyed talking to you.*"（很高興能和你聊天。）

Sixth Week, Third Day

An Invitation to Dinner

第六週，第三天 招待用餐

BASIC DIALOGUES

1. A : We're giving a small dinner party next Saturday night.
Can you make it?

下星期六我們要舉行一個小型宴會，你能來嗎？

B : Thank you. It's very nice of you to invite me. I'll
be glad to come.

謝謝你。你邀請我去，真是親切。我很樂意去。

2. A : Could you and your wife come to dinner this coming
Friday evening?

下個星期五晚上，你和你太太可以來吃晚飯嗎？

B : I'm sorry, but we have a previous engagement.

抱歉，不過我們已經先跟別人約好了。

3. A : Would Monday evening be convenient for you for dinner?

對你來說，星期一晚上方便來吃飯嗎？

B : Yes, it's most convenient for me, thanks.

是的，再方便也不過了，謝謝。

4. A : Thank you very much for inviting us to dinner today.

　　　非常謝謝你今天邀我們吃飯。

　　B : We're glad you could come. Please come in.

　　　我們很高興你們能來，請進。

5. A : *Everything is just delicious*. What a good cook you are!

　　　每樣東西眞的都很可口。你的烹調技術好棒哦！

　　B : Thanks for the compliment. I like to cook, you know.

　　　謝謝你的讚美。我喜歡烹調，你知道的。

6. A : That was certainly a delicious dinner. Thank you very much. 這一餐眞是美味。非常謝謝你。

　　B : You're quite welcome. We're glad you enjoyed it.

　　　不客氣。我們很高興你喜歡。

7. A : *Thank you for a very enjoyable evening.*

　　　謝謝你讓我有個非常愉快的夜晚。

　　B : We had a wonderful time, too.

　　　我們也渡過了一段美好的時光。

　　A : You must come to dinner at our house next time.

　　　下次你要來我們家吃晚飯。

　　B : Thank you. 謝謝你。

HINT BANK────────────

- *previous engagement* 先前的約會
- just 〔dʒʌst〕*adv*.〔口〕完全（= *quite*）；眞正地（= *really*）

* "I'll be glad to come." 這句話是以對方爲主體，使用 "come" 是表示「去那裏」的意思。
* 英美人對於別人的讚美，並不會覺得不好意思，通常會率直地回答："Thanks for the compliment."（謝謝你的讚美。）
* "Thank you for a very enjoyable evening." 這是拜訪者要告辭時，對主人所說的客套話。

◀ APPLIED CONVERSATION ▶ 邀請客人吃飯

Inviting Dinner Guests

喬　治： Hello, Peter. *I called to ask whether* you and your wife could have dinner with us next Sunday evening.

　　　　 嗨，彼得，我打電話來問，你和你太太下星期晚上是否可以和我們一起吃飯。

中國人： Well, thank you, George. Next Sunday evening? Let me see... that's the seventh, isn't it?

　　　　 嗯，謝謝你，喬治。下星期天晚上？我想想看…是七號，不是嗎？

喬　治： Yes, at about seven o'clock. 是的，大約七點左右。

中國人： I'm terribly sorry, George, we have another engagement for that evening.

　　　　 喬治，非常抱歉，那個晚上我們已經有約在先了。

喬　治： Then, how about a week from next Sunday? That will be the 14th. 那麼，下下星期天如何？那就是14號那一天。

中國人： That will be fine for me, but I'm afraid *I'm causing you a lot of trouble.*

　　　　 對我來說太好了，不過，恐怕會給你帶來很多麻煩。

HINT BANK ─────────────

* "Let me see."（讓我想想看。）也可以用 "Let's see." 來表示。
* "I'm terribly sorry." 句中的 "terribly" 是表示「非常」的口語用法。

喬　治：Not at all, Peter. I suppose your wife will be free
　　　　on that evening?
　　　　一點也不，彼得。我想你太太那天晚上會有空吧？

中國人：I'm sure she will, but perhaps I'd better ask her first.
　　　　Suppose I give you a call tomorrow morning. Will that
　　　　be all right? 我確信她會的，不過也許我最好先問她一聲。
　　　　我明天早上打通電話給你，這樣好不好？

喬　治：Certainly. 當然。

中國人：Incidentally, how about having lunch together today?
　　　　順便一提，今天一起吃午飯如何？

喬　治：Sure. Where shall we go? 當然，我們要去哪裏？

中國人：I have my car. Suppose I pick you up at your office
　　　　a little after 12 o'clock.
　　　　我有車。我十二點多到你的辦公室接你。

喬　治：That will be fine. I'll see you a little after twelve.
　　　　太好了。十二點多見。

中國人：Goodbye, George. 再見，喬治。

　　　　（Sound of receiver being replaced ／話筒放回去的聲音）----------
　　　　（Sound of phone bell ringing ／電話鈴響的聲音）----------

中國人：Mr. Lee speaking. 我姓李。

史密斯：Mr. Lee? This is William Smith.
　　　　李先生嗎？我是威廉・史密斯。

HINT BANK───────────────────────

　＊"Mr. Lee speaking." 這是講電話時的用語。在自己的姓之前加上 "Mr." 或
　　"Miss" 或 "Mrs." 是爲了向他人表示自己沒有 "Dr." 或其他頭銜之意。

中國人： How do you do, Mr. Smith？ 史密斯先生，你好嗎？

史密斯： I called you today to ask if you're free on the evening of the 14th. It's Sunday after next.
我今天打電話來，是請教十四號晚上你是否有空，就是下下星期天。

中國人： I'm so sorry, *I've just this minute accepted a dinner invitation* from a friend of mine.
很抱歉，我剛剛接受了一個朋友飯局的邀請。

史密斯： Oh, that's too bad. I should have called you a few minutes earlier. 喔，真可惜，我應該早幾分鐘打電話給你。

中國人： I certainly appreciate your invitation, Mr. Smith.
史密斯先生，我真的很感激你的邀請。

史密斯： *That's quite all right*, Mr. Lee. Perhaps some other time. 那兒的話，李先生，也許改天。

中國人： Yes, of course. Goodbye, Mr. Smith.
是的，當然。再見，史密斯先生。

史密斯： Goodbye, Mr. Lee. 再見，李先生。

HINT BANK ─────────────

· *this minute* 剛剛　　*some other time* 改天；過些時候

* " I should have called you～." 用 " should have ＋過去分詞 "的句型，是表示「應該做了（其實沒有）」的意思。

═Grammar and Usage═

1. 「吃」和「喝」的字彙

在英文中，表示「吃」是用"eat"，「喝」是用"drink"。但是，在日常的會話中，一般都用"*have*"來表示「吃」、「喝」的意思。

- I haven't *had* my breakfast yet.（我還沒吃早餐。）
- Won't you *have* another cup of tea?（要不要再喝一杯茶？）

另外，要注意，中國人所說的「喝湯」，在英文中，是用"*eat soup*"，而不是用"drink soup"。

2. "come"和"go"的用法

英文中的"come"，"go"與中文的「來」、「去」用法並不完全一樣。如：

- I'll be glad to *come*.（我很樂意去。）

中國人往往會說成"I'll be glad to go."之所以有這種差別，是因為英文用法把重點放在對方的立場。所以，往對方的方向，是用"come"而不是用"go"。如：

- George, come down quickly! — Yes, I'm *coming*.
- （喬治，快下來！　　　　　好，我來了。）

3. 在家款待客人

英美人習慣在自己的家中招待客人。這樣，不僅可以在愉快的氣氛中，談論各種話題，女主人也可以自己烹調菜餚來款待客人。

在他們的社交原則中，如果夫妻一起被邀請，二個人一定要一起赴宴。假如有一方不能參加，在禮貌上要婉拒這個邀請。另外，除了特別的情況之外，一般都不帶小孩子參加宴會。

Sixth Week, Fourth Day

Showing Someone around Famous Spots

第六週，第四天　陪某人遊覽名勝

BASIC DIALOGUES

1. A : *I'd be very happy if you could* show me around the city.
如果你能帶我參觀這個城市，我會非常高興。

　　B : Why, of course. I'll be glad to. 哦，當然，我很樂意。

2. A : *Have you ever been to* New York? 你到過紐約嗎？

　　B : No, I haven't. I'd like to go there sometime.
不，不曾。我想改天到那裏。

3. A : What would you like to see in Hengchun?
你想在恆春看到什麼？

　　B : I'd like to see Kenting Beach and Kenting Tropical Park.
我想看墾丁海水浴場和墾丁熱帶公園。

4. A : Could you take me to the National Palace Museum?
可否請你帶我去故宮？

　　B : Why, of course. It'll be a pleasure.
哦，當然，榮幸之至。

5. A： ***Are you acquainted with*** the Shihmen Dam?

你對石門水庫熟不熟？

B： Yes. I've seen it many times in photographs.

是的，我在照片裏頭看過很多次。

6. A： When was this structure built?這棟建築是什麼時候建造的？

B： The original was built during the Ching Dynasty, but it has been reconstructed several times since.

原來的建築是在清朝時建的，不過此後重建過很多次。

7. A： ***What is*** Fokuang Temple in Kaohsiung city ***famous for***?

高雄的佛光山以什麼聞名？

B： It's famous for its big statue of Buddha.

它是以巨大的佛像聞名。

8. A： Do I have to get permission to see the inside of this structure?光看這棟建築物的內部，我必須請求許可嗎？

B： No, you don't, but you must pay for an admission ticket at the entrance.

不，你不需要，不過你必須在入口處付門票錢。

9. A： Thank you so much for showing me around the city.

真謝謝你帶我參觀這個城市。

B： Not at all. It was a pleasure. 不客氣，榮幸之至。

HINT BANK ───────────────

- sometime〔'sʌm,taɪm〕*adv*. 改天　tropical〔'trɑpɪkl〕*adj*. 熱帶的
- ***acquaint with***～ 使熟悉；熟知　dynasty〔'daɪnəstɪ, 'daɪnæstɪ〕*n*. 朝代；王朝
- ***famous for***～ 以～聞名　***admission ticket*** 入場券；門票

* 問別人「有沒有到過～？」的句型是用 "Have you ever been to～?"也可用 "in"來代替"to"。

APPLIED CONVERSATION 到台北火車站接朋友
Meeting a Friend at Taipei Station

外國人：How do you do, Mr. Yang?
It was so nice of you to come
to the station to meet me.
楊先生，你好嗎？你到車站來
接我，眞是親切。

中國人：Not at all, Mr. Morgan. *I*
hope you had a nice trip.
不客氣，摩根先生。我希望你
有個愉快的旅程。

外國人：Very nice, thank you. 非常愉快，謝謝你。

中國人：I have a car waiting at the station entrance. We can
go to your hotel first.
我有車在車站大門的地方等著。我們可以先去你的旅館。

外國人：Good. Do you think we can begin sightseeing immediately? I'll just drop my bags at the hotel and register.
很好。你想我們是不是可以馬上開始觀光？我就把袋子放
在旅館，然後登記即可。

中國人：Of course we can, but aren't you tired?
當然可以，不過，你不累嗎？

HINT BANK———————————————

· register〔'redʒɪstə〕v.（在旅館的登記簿上）登記姓名（ = *check in*）

外國人：Not a bit. *I had a good night's rest*.

一點也不累。我昨晚充分地休息過。

中國人：Since you have only one suitcase, why don't we start our sightseeing tour right away? We can register at the hotel later. I've reserved a room for you.

既然你只有一個行李，我們何不立刻開始我們的觀光之旅？我們可以稍後再到旅館登記。我已經替你預訂了一個房間。

外國人：Good idea! Where do we go first?

好主意！我們先去什麼地方？

中國人：Well, since Lunshan District is so famous for its temples, I thought we might see a few of them this morning.

哦，龍山區的廟宇很有名，我想我們今天早上先去看看。

外國人：Of course. Which one shall we go to first?

當然。我們先去看那一座廟？

中國人：*Let me take you to* the Lunshan Temple. It is famous for stone sculptures.

我先帶你到龍山寺，它是以石雕聞名。

外國人：And from there? 然後呢？

中國人：From Lunshan Temple, we'll go to the Botanical Garden. It's famous for its lotuses.

我們從龍山寺到植物園。它是以荷花而聞名。

HINT BANK ─────────────

- sculpture〔'skʌlptʃɚ〕*n.* 雕刻；雕刻品
- lotus〔'lotəs〕*n.*〔植物〕蓮；荷

外國人： How interesting！那一定很有趣！

中國人： In the afternoon, we'll visit the Presidential Building.
I secured permission to enter the Presidential Building.
到了中午，我們就去參觀總統府。我已經得到進入總統府
的許可。

外國人： Oh, do you have to get permission to enter the Presidential Building? 喔，是不是要得到許可才能進入總統府？

中國人： Yes, I put in my application just as soon as I learned
you were coming down.
是的，我知道你要來，就馬上提出申請。

外國人： My, that was very thoughtful of you. 啊，你想得眞是周到。

中國人： Tomorrow we'll go to Tainan. Tainan is often called
the cradle of Taiwanese culture.
明天我們去台南。台南被稱爲台灣文化的搖籃。

外國人： What are some of the things we'll see in Tainan?
在台南我們會看些什麼？

中國人： We'll spend most of our time at the Confucian
Temple. It is the most famous Confucian Temple
in Taiwan.
我們大部分的時間會在孔廟。那是台灣最有名的孔廟。

HINT BANK

- secure〔sɪˈkjʊr〕 *v.* 得到；獲得　　***put in*** 提出證件；提出要求
- cradle〔ˈkredl〕 *n.* 搖籃；發源地

* "What are some of the things we'll see in Tainan?" 句中用 " some of "
是指「不能說是全部而是一部分」的意思。

外國人：Wonderful！ I've heard of Tainan's Confucian Temple before. 好極了！我以前曾聽過台南孔廟。

中國人：Well, shall we be on our way？
　　　哦，我們現在可以出發了嗎？

外國人：Yes, indeed. 是的，的確可以。

Sixth Week, Fifth Day

Hobbies

第六週,第五天 嗜好

BASIC DIALOGUES

1. A : *Do you have any hobbies*? 你有沒有任何嗜好?

   B : Yes, I have several hobbies. Music, reading, and stamp collecting. Besides them, I particularly like swimming and mountaineering.

   是的,我有幾個嗜好。音樂、閱讀、集郵。除此之外,我特別喜歡游泳和登山。

2. A : *What hobbies do you have*? 你有什麼嗜好?

   B : I'm afraid I don't have much time for hobbies.
   恐怕我沒有很多時間培養嗜好。

   A : That's too bad. You should develop a hobby. Hobbies take your mind off the worries of everyday life.
   太可惜了。你應該發展一種嗜好。嗜好釋去你心頭上日常生活的煩憂。

3. A：*Are you interested in anything in particular*？
　　　你有沒有特別對什麼感興趣？

　B：Music and sports are my hobbies. And how about you？
　　　音樂和運動是我的嗜好，你呢？

　A：My hobbies change every so often. Until a few months
　　　ago, pets were my hobby, but just now, I'm quite in-
　　　terested in oil painting.
　　　我的嗜好時常改變。到幾個月前為止，寵物是我的嗜好，不過
　　　現在，我對油畫相當有興趣。

4. A：I hear you have a big collection of LP records.
　　　聽說你收集了很多LP唱片。

　B：Not so big. Would you like to hear some？
　　　沒有那麼多，你要不要聽幾張？

　A：Yes, very much. 是的，非常想聽。

5. A：I'd like to see your collection of curios, if I may.
　　　如果可以的話，我想看你所收集的古董。

　B：I'd be most happy if you did.
　　　如果你想看的話，我再樂意也不過了。

6. A：Where have you been？
　　　你到過哪些地方？

HINT BANK

　· mountaineering〔‚maʊntə'nɪrɪŋ〕*n.* 登山
　· *every so often* 時常（ = *every now and then* = *every once in a while*）
　· *LP record* 三十三轉唱片；長時間唱片（＝Long Playing or 33⅓ RPM record）
　· curio〔'kjʊrɪ‚o〕*n.* 古董

B： I've been to the museum. A fine collection of modern French paintings are now on display.

我到過博物館。現在正展示大量收集的法國現代畫。

7. A： I'm going to the movies. Won't you come with me？

我要去看電影，跟我去好嗎？

B： I'd be glad to. What are you going to see？

我很樂意，你要看哪一部？

A： A new comedy. We can't miss it.

一部新的喜劇，我們決不能錯過。

HINT BANK ─────────────────────────

• fine〔faɪn〕*adj.* 廣大的（= *extensive*）

• museum〔mjuˊziəm〕*n.* 博物館；〔美〕美術館（= *art museum*）

◀ APPLIED CONVERSATION ▶　談論嗜好

Talking about Hobbies

中國人： Hello, Jack. 嗨，傑克。

傑　克： Hello, Mei-mei. Come on in.
Laura and David are here.
嗨，美美，請進。羅拉和大衞
都在這裏。

中國人： Hello, Laura. How are you,
David?
嗨，羅拉。大衞，你好嗎？

羅　拉： Hello, Mei-mei. 嗨，美美。

大　衞： How have you been, Mei-mei? 美美，近來好嗎？

中國人： Fine. *What are you all doing*? 很好，你們都在做什麼？

傑　克： Oh, we've been talking about hobbies.
喔，我們在談嗜好。

大　衞： Yes, Jack was telling us that his hobby is collecting
stamps.
是的，傑克告訴我們，他的嗜好是集郵。

HINT BANK ────────────────────────

* " How have you been? " （近來如何？）這是 " How are you? " 的現在完成
式。
* " What are you all doing? " 句中的 " you all " 是指「你們各位；大家」的意
思。

中國人： Yes, you showed me your stamp collection one day, didn't you?

是的，你有一天給我看過你收集的郵票，不是嗎？

大　衛： How about you, Mei-mei？ Do you have a hobby?

美美，你呢？你有嗜好嗎？

中國人： I like to do so many things that I don't have a regular hobby. Just now I'm interested in embroidery!

我喜歡做的事情太多了，所以我沒有固定的嗜好。我目前對刺繡有興趣。

羅　拉： My, how nice! That's one of my hobbies, too. But *I don't take my hobbies as seriously as David*.

哇，太棒了！那也是我的嗜好之一，但是，我沒有像大衛那麼正經地把它當做我的嗜好。

中國人： Oh? And what's your hobby, David?

喔？大衛，你的嗜好是什麼？

大　衛： Oh, I'm interested in models... like trains, and air-planes and boats.

喔，我對模型有興趣…像火車、飛機跟船。

傑　克： I didn't know that, David. Do you buy those model kits that they sell?

大衛，我對這個不清楚。你買那些他們賣的模型組嗎？

HINT BANK————————————————

· *one day* （過去或未來的）有一天　　*just now* （現在式）目前；（過去式）方才
· embroidery〔ɪmˈbrɔɪdərɪ〕*n.* 刺繡　　kit〔kɪt〕*n.*〔俗〕一組

* “ those model kits that they sell ” 句中的 “ they ” 是指「 商店裏的人 」。

大　衛：No, they aren't much fun. I like to make my own
　　　　models. 不，那些沒有多大樂趣。我喜歡自己做模型。

羅　拉：Yes, he ***spends hours and hours*** making all kinds of
　　　　things. I must say he's quite clever at it. Some of
　　　　his models have won prizes.
　　　　是的，他花很多時間在做各式各樣的東西，我必須說他相當
　　　　擅長於此。他做的有些模型曾經得獎。

中國人：Really？真的嗎？

傑　克：You know Michelle, don't you？ She has a wonderful
　　　　collection of " Zombie " dolls.
　　　　你認識蜜雪兒，不是嗎？她收集了一些很棒的「僵屍」娃娃。

中國人：Yes, I've seen her collection. It's very large. She
　　　　must have at least a hundred different dolls.
　　　　是的，我看過她的收集。很龐大，她至少一定有一百個不同
　　　　的娃娃。

羅　拉：I thought of collecting " Zombie " dolls for a hobby
　　　　too, but I became more interested in embroidery.
　　　　我也想過以收集「僵屍」娃娃作爲嗜好，但是，我對刺繡比
　　　　較感興趣。

大　衛：Well, ***I suppose it doesn't matter what your hobbies
　　　　are as long as you have one***.
　　　　嗯，我想，你的嗜好是什麼都沒關係，祇要有一個嗜好就可以了。

傑　克：Yes, you're right. 是的，你說得不錯。

HINT BANK────────────────────

- ***be clever at*** 擅長於
- zombi〔'zɑmbɪ〕*n.* 僵屍

Sixth Week, Sixth Day

An Invitation to a Party

第六週，第六天 邀請參加舞會

BASIC DIALOGUES

1. A : Next Saturday is my birthday, and I'm having a little party at my house. You'll be able to come, won't you ?

下個星期六是我的生日，我在家舉行一個小型宴會，你可以來，不是嗎？

B : Thank you very much. I'll be glad to come.

非常謝謝你，我很樂意去。

2. A : Did you receive an invitation to Mr. Kent's party ?

你收到肯特先生宴會的邀請嗎？

B : Yes, I did, and I've just answered the invitation. You're going too, aren't you ?

是的，我收到了，而且我剛剛已經回覆了這個邀請，你也要去，不是嗎？

A : It's a shame, but I can't. *I sent my regrets.*

真可惜，我不能去，我已經寄了辭謝函。

B： I'm sorry to hear that. 聽到這樣，眞是遺憾。

3. A： May I take you to the dance？ 我帶你去參加舞會好嗎？

B： Yes, of course. I'd love to go. 好，當然，我很樂意去。

4. A： *May I have this dance, please*？ 這支曲子我可以跟你共舞嗎？

B： Certainly. 好的。

5. A： May I have the next dance, please？
下一支曲子我可以跟你共舞嗎？

B： I'm sorry. I've already promised it to Fred.
抱歉，我已經答應弗瑞德了。

6. A： What will you have to drink？ 你要喝什麼？

B： I'll have a dry martini. 我喝不加苦艾的馬丁尼。

7. A： Thanks so much. I've had a wonderful time.
非常謝謝，我渡過了一段美好的時光。

B： We're so glad you could come. 我們很高興你能來。

8. A： John, will you please escort Mary home？
約翰，請你送瑪莉回家好嗎？

B： Why, of course. It'll be a pleasure.
哦，當然，榮幸之至。

HINT BANK

- regret〔rɪ'grɛt〕 n.（對於邀請等的）辭謝（函）　dance〔dæns〕 n. 舞會
- dry〔draɪ〕 adj.（雞尾酒）未加苦艾酒的
- martini〔mɑr'tinɪ〕 n. 馬丁尼酒（一種以苦艾酒和苦橘爲主要成分的雞尾酒）
- escort〔'ɛskɔrt〕 v. 護送

* " It's a shame." 句中的 " shame " 本來是「羞恥」的意思，在此是當「遺憾」
（ = *pity* ）的意思。

❌APPLIED CONVERSATION❌ 在生日舞會中
At a Birthday Party

海　倫：Hello, Mei-mei. I'm so glad
you could come.
嗨！美美，我眞高興你能來。

中國人：Thanks for inviting me. And
happy birthday, Helen.
謝謝你邀請我。生日快樂，海
倫。

海　倫：Thank you. 謝謝你。

中國人：Here, *I brought a little gift
for you*. 嘿，我有一個小禮物要送給你。

海　倫：Oh, thank you so much. Come on in and take off your
coat. The others are in the big room. Here, let me
have your coat.
噢，眞謝謝你！請進來，把外套脫掉。其他人在大廳。來，
把外套給我。

中國人：Thanks. Is everyone here already?
謝謝。每個人都來了嗎？

海　倫：I believe a few more will be coming. I think you know
everybody here.
我想還有幾個人會來。我想這裡的每個人你都認識。

HINT BANK

* " a little gift for you " 英美人在送別人禮物時，常會加個 " little " 這個字。

中國人： Yes, I think so. 是的，我想是的。

約　翰： Hello, Mei-mei. *Did you just get here*?
嗨，美美，你剛到嗎？

中國人： Yes, I just came. My, there's quite a crowd here!
是的，我剛到。哇啊！這裏聚集了好多人！

約　翰： There certainly is... just about everybody we know.
的確…幾乎我們所認識的每一個人都來了。

中國人： Oh, there's Sally over there.
喔，莎莉在那邊。

莎　莉： Oh, hello, Mei-mei. How have you been?
喔，嗨，美美，你好嗎？

中國人： Fine, thanks. And you?
很好，謝謝。你呢？

莎　莉： Oh, I've been quite well. Oh, John, will you get Mei-mei something to drink?
哦，我非常的好。哦，約翰，拿杯飲料給美美好嗎？

約　翰： Of course. What would you like, Mei-mei?
當然好。美美，你喜歡喝什麼？

（Dance music fades in. ／跳舞音樂漸漸響起。）----------

HINT BANK

· *fade in*（電影、無線電及電視中之）漸強

＊ " There certainly is "這是附和別人的用法。

中國人：Let me see... I think I'll have some ginger ale.
我想想看…我想喝薑汁汽水。

約　翰：How about a cocktail？
雞尾酒如何？

中國人：Yes, if you can make me one that isn't too strong.
好啊！如果你能爲我調杯不太强的雞尾酒。

約　翰：OK. I'll get a manhattan for you.
沒問題。我調杯曼哈坦雞尾酒給你。

中國人：Oh, hello, Fred. It's nice to see you again.
喔，嗨，弗瑞德，再次見到你眞好。

弗瑞德：It's nice to see you, Mei-mei. Would you like to dance？
很高興見到你，美美。你想跳舞嗎？

中國人：Later, if you don't mind. I'm waiting for John to
bring me a drink.
如果你不介意的話，我們待會兒再跳。我在等約翰替我拿飲
料來。

弗瑞德：Of course, Mei-mei.
沒問題，美美。

中國人：Look！ *Doesn't Helen look lovely in that blue dress*？
你看！海倫穿那套藍色禮服看起來不是很漂亮嗎？

HINT BANK────────────

- ginger〔'dʒɪndʒɚ〕n. 薑
- manhattan〔mæn'hætn〕n. 曼哈坦雞尾酒（裸麥威士忌或巴本威士忌加淡的或甜的艾酒而成）

莎　莉： She certainly does.
　　　　的確漂亮。

約　翰： Here's your drink, Mei-mei.
　　　　你的飲料來了，美美。

中國人： Oh, thank you so much, John. Shall we go over in the corner so we won't be in the way of the dancing？
　　　　喔，非常謝謝你，約翰。我們到那邊的角落去，免得妨礙別人跳舞，好嗎？

約　翰： Yes. *How about the next dance*？
　　　　好。下一支曲子和我一起跳好嗎？

中國人： I'd love to.
　　　　我很樂意。

HINT BANK ─────────────────

・ *in the way* 妨礙

革命性英語學習新方法

說英文高手①

➤ **劉 毅 編著**

　　劉　毅老師繼「一天背好 1000 個英單字」後，又有一個革命性的新發明。「說英文高手①」出版後，即造成轟動。

☆ 三句爲一組，一次説三句 ☆

　　人類的短暫記憶有限，如這個數字「411213311」很難背，但是分開來，「411－213－311」就較容易背。如再排成「211－311－411」就不可能忘記。英文一句一句背，容易忘記，但是一次背三句相關連的句子，就不容易忘。

☆ 容易記，不容易忘 ☆

　　「説英文高手」的句子，都是摘錄自美國人常用的會話，而且隨時可用得到，可以和外國人説，可以和中國人説，也可以自言自語説。例如：你隨時可説："What a beauitful day it is !"（多麼美好的一天！）再接著説：It's not too hot. It's not too cold. It's just right. 像這樣的句子，就是容易記、不容易忘，隨時可以用得到。

☆ 跟著錄音帶説，效果特佳 ☆

　　「説英文高手」錄音帶的製作，以三句爲一組，第一次先用慢速，你可跟著外國老師唸。第二次用正常速度，一次唸三句。最後一次用正常速度唸完整個單元。只要利用上下班的時間，或等公車的時間，聽聽錄音帶，跟著唸，很快地你就可以一次説三句以上，成爲説英文高手。你的朋友見到你會説：

Your English is improving.
Your English is progressing.
Your English is getting better.

◉ 書*180*元 ╱ 錄音帶四卷*500*元

全省各大書局均售

|||||||||||||| ● 學習出版公司門市部 ● ||||||||||||||

台北地區：台北市許昌街 10 號 2 樓 TEL：(02)3314060・3319209
台中地區：台中市綠川東街 32 號 8 樓 23 室
TEL：(04)2232838

|||||||||||||||||||||||||||||||||||||||||||||||||

六週美語會話

編　　　著 / 林　婷
發　行　所 / 學習出版有限公司　　　　　　　☎ (02) 7045525
郵 撥 帳 號 / 0512727-2 學習出版社帳戶
登　記　證 / 局版台業 2179 號
印　刷　所 / 裕強彩色印刷有限公司
台 北 門 市 / 台北市許昌街 10 號 2 F　　　　☎ (02) 3314060・3319209
台 中 門 市 / 台中市綠川東街 32 號 8 F 23 室　☎ (04) 2232838
台灣總經銷 / 學英文化事業公司　　　　　　　☎ (02) 2187307
美國總經銷 / Evergreen Book Store　　　　　☎ (818) 2813622

售價：新台幣一百五十元正

1997 年 11 月 1 日一版四刷

ISBN 957-519-030-0